LITTLE,
BROWN

LARGE
PRINT

The TWELVE Topsy-Turvy, Very Messy DAYS of CHRISTMAS

JAMES PATTERSON
and TAD SAFRAN

LITTLE, BROWN AND COMPANY

LARGE PRINT EDITION

Copyright © 2022 by James Patterson

Hachette Book Group supports the right to free expression and the value of copyright. The purpose of copyright is to encourage writers and artists to produce creative works that enrich our culture.

The scanning, uploading, and distribution of this book without permission is a theft of the author's intellectual property. If you would like permission to use material from the book (other than for review purposes), please contact permissions@hbgusa.com. Thank you for your support of the author's rights.

Little, Brown and Company
Hachette Book Group
1290 Avenue of the Americas, New York, NY 10104

First edition: October 2022

Little, Brown and Company is a division of Hachette Book Group, Inc. The Little, Brown name and logo are trademarks of Hachette Book Group, Inc.

The publisher is not responsible for websites (or their content) that are not owned by the publisher.

The Hachette Speakers Bureau provides a wide range of authors for speaking events. To find out more, go to hachettespeakersbureau.com or call (866) 376-6591.

Interior book design by Marie Mundaca

ISBN 9780316405904 (hc) / 9780316474429 (large print)

LCCN 2022941580

Printing 1, 2022

LSC-C

Printed in the United States of America

The TWELVE Topsy-Turvy, Very Messy DAYS of CHRISTMAS

The Day Before the First Day

Chapter 1

WHAT IS THE worst present you ever received for Christmas?

A pair of socks?

A pair of scratchy socks in a vile color?

A pair of scratchy socks in a disgusting color that rub your big toes every step you take?

A pair of coarse socks in a foul color that rub your big toes and you're forced to wear them because your grandmother gave them to you and she's coming to stay?

That's pretty bad. But for Will and Ella Sullivan, the worst thing they ever got for Christmas was a dead mother. Apologies for going so dark before the first page is even over. Apologies if, in your shock, you allowed your cookie to plop into your milk. But the simple truth is, people die every day. Statistically speaking, *someone* unfortunately has to die on Christmas Day. For Will and Ella Sullivan, it was their mother.

So when Christmas rolls around—as it does every year—and all the houses on a particular modestly gentrified Harlem street are festooned with Christmas lights and decorations, one large, decaying Victorian house with chipping paint remains unadorned. This is the house where Will and Ella Sullivan live with their father, Henry. It remains an island of somber darkness that seems to deny the existence of Christmas, fortified by a seasonal gloom against any encroachment of jollity that may try to breach its borders. For at this time of year in the Sullivan house, stockings go unstuffed, tinsel unstrewn, gifts unbought, mistletoe unhung, chestnuts unroasted, carols unplayed, cookies uncooked, and a tree unvisible.

Not only did Will and Ella lose their mother five years ago, they also lost Christmas. (To be absolutely clear, though, they didn't *technically* lose their mother. They know exactly where she is. In a tastefully decorated burial plot in the cemetery. At least, she'd better be there because, if she's not, she's a zombie or something and these poor children—who have surely suffered enough—risk being subjected to a whole different kind of emotional trauma.)

The house itself is not to blame. It was built in another century—pre-TV and internet, if you can imagine such barbarous times—with adequate rooms and space to absorb the bustle, noises, and smells associated with a busy, vibrant family who had to amuse themselves without the help of Instagram or Netflix.

It was the generous proportions and original features of the house that attracted Henry and Katie Sullivan. It certainly wasn't the colony of obstinate mice who had taken up residence. Or the peeling wallpaper. Or the pipes that rattled and popped when faucets were turned on. And off. Or the kitchen full of the most modern, space-age, and technically advanced appliances that money could buy...during the presidency of Dwight D. Eisenhower.

Despite those negatives, which had chased

away all previous sane potential buyers, Henry and Katie Sullivan knew the house was the one for them the moment that they walked in with little Will and Ella toddling around their knees. The task ahead of them was daunting, but they would have a lifetime to fix it up.

Unfortunately, "a lifetime" in this case was to be just four short years.

Not knowing they had so little time, Henry and Katie slowly did what they could afford to do to make the old house a home. Modern plumbing and moderately priced new appliances were a good start. And new paint, rugs, curtains, and comfortable furniture went a long way to brightening up the place.

But the key ingredients were love and laughter. You may not know this, but it's an accepted fact that no room is completely done until furnished with a child's giggle. And there was no shortage of those at the Sullivan household.

While Henry was responsible for most of the work on the interior of the house, Katie spent her time outside. Not because she'd forgotten her key or wasn't house-trained. But because the house had an unusually large walled private garden behind it. Big enough for flower beds, vegetable patches, paths, trees, and a fountain. Big enough for children to play long, exhausting games of tag or even hide-and-seek. This was where Will and Ella's mother spent her days and her energy, up to her elbows and ankles in soil, turning the overgrown, muddy patch of scrubland into an Eden.

A unique, jazzlike energy and rhythm had surrounded the four Sullivans whenever they were all together, which was almost constantly. But after their mother's death, that energy and rhythm ground to a halt as the ensemble, over the weeks and months, drifted apart.

Those happy days seemed like a long time ago to Will and Ella, who each now retained a diminishing number of increasingly foggy memories from those laughter-filled years. And Will and Ella, who had once been as thick as thieves, had grown apart... Will having grown louder and Ella having grown quieter.

Nowadays, even when they were technically

together, they were essentially apart. Mealtimes were quiet affairs with tepid food and equally tepid conversation, to be endured rather than enjoyed as they had been in the past.

Restaurants, movie theaters, clothing shops, candy stores, and parks—in addition to Christmas—became luxuries for other people and not for the Sullivans. As did hugs, understanding, enthusiasm, and a general interest in one another's thoughts, dreams, and problems.

Unable to confront his own emotions, Henry was tragically unequipped to understand his children's. Not that he felt he ever had time to try. He was at his wit's end just keeping them fed, watered, clothed, healthy, educated, safe, and largely polite.

'The lovely, large garden behind the house had two entrances. A back door allowed access from the kitchen, and a gate allowed entry from the alley that ran alongside the house. Soon after his wife's death, Henry added a heavy dead bolt to the first and a foreboding padlock to the second. As with so many parts of his life that he had once enjoyed, Henry now ignored the garden. He was too sad to cultivate it himself and too protective to let anyone else. Untended, it soon grew dark and wild, which is nature's way with almost anything that doesn't receive the attention it craves.

Chapter 2

THE EL GRANDE is a large department store in lower Harlem that has withstood the changing demographics of the local population. One of the reasons for its longevity is its long-standing reputation of offering good value on life's necessities.

A group of four boys, aged sixteen years old, certainly thought so. They milled about, intent on taking advantage of Christmas bargains. Bargains that the store, however, had not anticipated. Cuz, Bean, Fash, and Noodle had been friends since they met in detention several years ago. They were brought together by a shared love of rule-breaking, baggy clothes, beanie hats, and odd nicknames.

When Cuz entered the store, he was athletic

and trim, verging on skinny. But the more he walked around the aisles with his friends, the fatter he seemed to become. Soon his long coat bulged and strained until he resembled a textbook candidate for type 2 diabetes. In fact, he looked a lot like his friend Noodle, who was born weighing an eye-watering fourteen pounds and hadn't met a morsel of food since then that he didn't like.

Noticing this unusual group of boys shopping as a pack, a keen-eyed sales assistant made his way toward them. Before he could get there, however, he was spotted by another, younger boy standing on the other side of the department.

This boy was about fourteen years old but smallish for his age. He had a mop of unruly dark-blond hair that he regularly pushed out of his face and keen, darting, light-brown eyes that turned green in certain lights and moods. This boy was Will Sullivan. Pulling his hoodie up over his head, he smiled his trademark mischievous grin and kicked the bottom suitcase in an oversize tower of luggage. The stack promptly toppled over with an almighty crash, taking with it two racks of reasonably priced sunglasses.

The moment they heard the noise and saw that the sales assistant's attention was diverted, the group of boys knew it was time to get out of there. They ran. And were soon joined by Will.

"Stop them! There! Those boys!" the sales assistant shouted to the security guard, who immediately chased after them. The guard had been a sprinter in high school fifteen years ago. And he was determined not to let the blue polyester uniform pants that clung annoyingly to his thick thighs hamper his thief-catching abilities.

The boys skidded down aisles and through departments. Hot on their heels was the security guard like a lion after a group of gazelles...who had stolen from the lion. Running down escalators, they knocked shoppers out of the way until they burst out of the shop and into the bitterly cold New York afternoon as if shot from a cannon.

Cuz reached into his coat and pulled out a couple of T-shirts. He thrust them into

Will's hand and said, "Good job, Will." The other boys patted Will on the back. Bean gave him a playful punch on the arm, which actually hurt quite a lot, but Will grinned through the pain, happy to be one of the gang. His enjoyment was cut short when the security guard skidded out of the store and spotted them.

"Everybody split up," barked Fash.

With that, the gang dispersed in all directions. The last one to go was Will, who was hurriedly trying to unlock his bike from a railing, but his cold, anxious fingers seemed to have a mind of their own. Finally, just as the security guard was reaching out for him, Will whipped his bike away, swung a leg over it, and pedaled away as fast as he could. As he disappeared around the corner, Will looked over his shoulder at the gasping security guard and gave a cheeky little wave.

If he hadn't turned around to give that unnecessary wave, Will might have seen the pretzel cart right in front of him. As it was, he didn't and, spotting it only at the very last moment, swerved, pinballing his bike from a wall into a lamppost and down to the ground. Hard.

Will lay there for a moment as pedestrians, muttering at the inconvenience, stepped over and around him. He painfully picked himself up and limped away with his bike, disappearing into the crowds before the security guard could see that his quarry had been injured. Will had luckily escaped with nothing more than a few minor scrapes.

His bike, on the other hand, had not been so fortunate. The frame was bent to such a degree that it looked like it had been specifically designed for cycling around corners. He silently cursed pretzel carts and street vendors as a whole for destroying his sole means of transportation and freedom. This was clearly their fault and not his.

Dragging his crooked bike the rest of the way home through the gritty grayness of Harlem in December, Will grappled with how he might explain the dilapidated state of the bike to his father. But he was soon distracted by pleasanter thoughts. As he passed houses, Will found himself craning his neck to look through their windows. He observed the lush Christmas trees colorfully hung with baubles and tinsel. He saw extravagantly wrapped gifts piled high under trees. He saw long, thick stockings hanging from mantels and smelled the cookies baking in kitchens. He sighed deeply.

Chapter 3

CARELESSLY GATHERING DUST on shelves in Henry Sullivan's small, dark, cluttered Columbia University office was an eclectic collection of items from his travels, mainly with Katie, who had encouraged Henry to overcome his innate frugality to acquire fascinating and rare artifacts. Among them, you would find a large carved stone snake head that once adorned an Incan palace, a block of jet-black lava rock from Hawaii, a taxidermy armadillo in a particularly ferocious pose, a smooth (much used) Fijian war club, and a pair of long wooden poles topped with baskets that farmers in nineteenth-century England used to pluck apples from high branches. It was a collection that might bring any antiquarian joy—especially a professor of history like Henry—but Henry hadn't looked at the items in years.

Instead, absently finishing off a small glass of bourbon, he stared at the stack of exam booklets looming on his desk before him. In truth, Henry did not look out of place among all the other worn and obsolete curiosities that populated his office. In their prime, all the objects had been fine examples of what they were. Likewise, Henry had been a fine example of a young man. Vibrant, tall, and square-shouldered with a physique that appeared more athletic than his abilities warranted. He'd had a sharp wit and a boyish laugh. But now his dusty blond hair was thinner and unkempt, his jacket was frayed, his tie was stained, his beard was scraggly, and his warm blue eyes, dulled by time and worry, were not as shiny as they had once been.

He took a deep breath and opened the top exam booklet. Having read a few lines, he gently massaged his temples. Then, without reading another word, he took the top off his red pen and began to rapidly and randomly mark up the pages. He put a question mark here and an exclamation point there. He circled paragraphs and wrote intelligent-sounding words like *trite, lazy,* or *conjecture* at regular intervals until he arrived at the last page, where he scrawled "C+" and closed the book.

Satisfied that the whole process had taken less than a minute, he grabbed a second and third and fourth exam booklet and did likewise until he was interrupted by a knock on the door.

"Come in!" Henry shouted.

The door opened and in strode a broad-shouldered man, slightly older than Henry, with a melodious voice and electric smile that warmed any room.

"Henry, my boy," he boomed.

"Hastie," Henry greeted his friend, who, despite his name, moved quite slowly. Henry continued, "To what do I owe the honor?" and motioned for Hastie to take a seat opposite him.

Dr. Hastings Fringe gently lowered himself into the cracked leather chair with a brief, involuntary groan. Fixing his deep brown eyes on Henry, Dr. Fringe ran a massive hand over his springy mane of gray and black hair that added at least two inches to his height. After taking a moment to decide how to begin, Dr. Fringe finally came out with it.

"Henry, did you, um…did you *discuss* Dean Grumpf's new book in your class?"

"I did."

"Okay. Okay. Um, what exactly did you say about it? Nothing… *bad,* right?"

"Not at all," Henry reassured Dr. Fringe, who was in fact provost of the college and the world's greatest living authority on the Beer Act of 1830, an obscure but fascinating piece of parliamentary legislation that laid the groundwork for some of the great liberal reforms of law and society in nineteenth-century Britain.

"Oh, good." Dr. Fringe let out a relieved laugh while removing his glasses and polishing the lenses with a large red-polka-dotted handkerchief. "So glad we cleared that up."

"I, uh…I might have mentioned, however," Henry continued, "that his premise was entirely false, built upon implausible hypotheses and lazy research."

Dr. Fringe rubbed his eyes. "When you say you 'might have mentioned' it, what exactly do you mean?"

"I mean that...I dedicated roughly thirty minutes of my class to a thorough verbal shredding of every word printed in his book."

"Henry!" Dr. Fringe exclaimed in a chastising, exasperated manner. "You just said you didn't say anything bad about it."

"It's not *bad* if it's *true*," Henry countered.

"You are aware that Dean Grumpf is the head of your department. And is responsible for the hiring and firing of his professors?"

"And I'm responsible for the education of my students."

Dr. Fringe looked skeptically over the top of his clean glasses at Henry.

"Hastie," Henry leaned forward in his chair, "the book is drivel. I'm not kidding. It's an insult to paper."

"At least he's published," Dr. Fringe pointedly pointed out. "Where's *your* book?"

This was clearly a sore subject for Henry,

who retreated into his seat. Years ago, during a trip with Katie to the Dominican Republic, he had discovered a cache of never-before-studied letters in a dilapidated library. They were written by one of Napoleon's generals and cast a revolutionary and critical light on the emperor's legendary military abilities.

Henry had been three-quarters of the way through writing his groundbreaking, revisionist history of Napoleon when Katie died. In fact, he had printed out the pages just that morning. Needless to say, he never picked those pages up off the printer and couldn't tell you whatever happened to them.

"If you had just finished and published your book, *you'd* be dean right now instead of Grumpf. I wish it had been you. I genuinely do. But that's not what happened."

From the moment he was made dean, Vilander Grumpf wanted Henry's head on a platter. Not literally. That would be far too messy. And, quite frankly, difficult to explain to friends and visitors when they arrive at your house and see a severed head on a shiny tray dripping blood onto the floor in the entrance hall. Grumpf simply didn't like having Henry around. It reminded him of the fact that he only held his position because it slipped through someone else's fingers.

"He is your boss, Henry. And you don't publicly insult your boss. Not if you like having a job...no matter how right you may be...which I'm not saying you are...although I did read a few pages of Grumpf's book and am not unsympathetic to your point of view." He paused, then added forcefully, "But that's not the point!"

"It'll all blow over, Hastie," Henry said with a shrug.

"Not this time. He has demanded that we convene a disciplinary peer review."

"A disciplinary review?!" Henry exclaimed, suddenly grasping the gravity of the situation. "Is that really necessary?"

"Your department head seems to think so and it's his call."

As Dr. Fringe hoisted himself out of his chair, he looked at Henry's unkempt hair, heavily lidded eyes, and carelessly trimmed beard. He looked at the accumulation of dust on the cluttered desk and the messy pile of exam papers topped by a glistening empty glass.

"Have you been drinking?"

"No," replied Henry, pushing his desk drawer shut with a soft rattling of bottles.

Chapter 4

BUT WHERE WAS the third Sullivan who resided in that quiet, unadorned, empty house
in Harlem?

In the house, actually.

In her room, to be more precise. Unseen.
Not noticed. Which was par for the course,
since most people didn't notice Ella. Had
anyone actually taken the time to look at
her, they would have seen a tall, slender girl
with expressive blue eyes and a shy but bright
smile. At least that is what they would have
seen had she stood up straight, brushed her
long black hair out of her face, and actually
made eye contact with them.

But she didn't and so they wouldn't. And
that was the way she liked it. Or, at least,

everything that she did would lead an observer to believe that that is the way she liked it. But, deep down, the truth was that she was simply worried by what people would see if they noticed her.

Would they, like the confident girls in school, make fun of her hair that just hung there without bounce or style? Would they disapprovingly scrunch up their faces at the dark, shapeless clothes that she wore? Or would they take offense at something she said that was taken out of context? It seemed to Ella that being seen was just not worth the risk. And, as you'll learn, avoiding risk was of paramount importance to Ella.

Ella's room was clean. Not *clean* like she made her bed and put away her toys. Clean, like a hospital operating room designed by a Scandinavian minimalist Buddhist monk with a crate of bleach wipes that were about to expire.

The fact was, soon after her mother's death, the thought of germs and the appearance of anything out of place began to irk Ella. It started small. Toys, dolls, and crayons needed to be put in drawers and surfaces needed to be free of obvious dirt. But before long, all items deemed "unnecessary" were ruthlessly discarded, counters were disinfected multiple times each day, clothes were folded to exact dimensions, and books were arranged by color and height, their glossy covers having been studiously wiped clean. Clutter and disorder were where bacteria and disease could live and spread, and Ella could not allow that.

She took it upon herself to keep all common areas of the dark old house obsessively disinfected. None of the furnishings, curtains, or decor had been upgraded since her mother's death, and they were therefore showing signs of age and wear. Ella couldn't help that. But what she could do was make sure they were sanitized, cleansed, and, where possible, sterilized to the best of her germ-fighting ability. Her bedroom, however, became Ella's special sanctuary of pristine cleanliness.

Ella squirted hand sanitizer into her palm and rubbed her hands together, looking at her paintbrushes, which were all lined up and evenly spaced on a piece of paper towel. Picking up the brush farthest to the left, she swirled it in a glass of clear water and dabbed it on the square of brown paint. She then applied the brown watercolor paint to the clean white paper held in her tidy wooden easel. She looked out of the window and, in measured strokes, lost herself in capturing the untamed, twisting foliage of the garden behind the house.

Her peaceful world, however, was soon rudely shattered by the noise of her brother, Will, bursting into her room. Wherever Ella was, she desired quiet. Wherever Will went, he created noise. Such was the yin and yang of these siblings.

"Knock, Will! You knock before you enter a room," Ella instructed. "And take your filthy shoes off!"

Kicking off his sneakers, Will rapped his knuckles twice on her forehead. "Knock knock."

"Get off!" Ella pushed him away.

Will sat on the bed, creating creases that caused Ella to wince.

"Open up the website. Go on. Open it up. Come on."

Ella paused, looking at her brother's annoying, eager face. She knew he wouldn't let it go and would keep pestering her until she did as he asked. So, with deliberate slowness, she carefully cleaned and placed her paintbrush back where it had been next to the others and reached for her laptop. As she opened it up, the computer *zoinnnnng*ed to life.

Chapter 5

On-screen was Splice.com, a dating website that described itself as "a site for people specifically interested in marriage."

You might think that Will and Ella—being fourteen and twelve years old—were too young to be interested in marriage. But you'd be wrong. They were *very* interested in marriage. The sooner the better. Not for *themselves,* you weirdo. Is that where your mind went? No, they were interested in marriage for their *father.*

The fact was, Will and Ella wanted their father to be happy. Why? Was it because they cared about his fragile emotional state and general decline since the death of their mother? In part, maybe, yes. But mainly it was because the last time *they had Christmas* was when he was happy. And the last time he was happy was when he was married. So, they figured, the best way to get Christmas—and more crucially, Christmas *presents*—back was to get their father married.

They had gone as far as creating the profile page for Henry, using a photo from seven years ago when Henry's hair was a little thicker and his waist was a little thinner. They'd already filled out most of the questions on his behalf but were now focusing on the "interests" section.

After a certain amount of debate, Ella typed in *tango dancing, car racing, and nineteenth-century romantic poetry.* The siblings were aware that they were stretching the truth somewhat, but they couldn't put *complaining about the neighbors, TV watching, and getting annoyed with his children.*

And anyway, they justified, the "interests" they put in were based in truth. Their father had performed something approximating a tango dance when Will spilled a box of thumbtacks on the floor where Henry was passing barefoot. And he did drive too fast, generally speaking. And just the other day, Henry had pulled a thick poetry book off the shelf...and put it under the broken leg of the TV console. So they weren't *total* lies.

Their biggest worry, though, was how to pay the subscription required by the website. They could build Henry's profile, but no potential wives could communicate with them until they had actually activated the account with a credit card...which neither of them had. Will told Ella not to worry about it. When the profile was ready to go, he'd think of something. Probably stealing Henry's credit card and hoping he never noticed the $8.99 charge each month from Splice.com.

"Are you sure we're doing the right thing? Going behind his back and all?" Ella asked.

"Do you want Christmas presents or not?" Will responded.

She did. That was the whole point of this exercise. Will and Ella wanted presents. They *deserved* presents. They were going to get presents.

"When he's married and we have Christmas again," Ella dreamed, "what present do you want?"

"*Present?* Singular? Are you crazy? I'm not doing this for one stinking present. I want lots. This year, Cuz's parents are getting him a new PlayStation, a TV for his own bedroom, Bose headphones, and a week at rock camp."

"Sounds like his parents just want him to stay away from them," Ella pointed out. "And I don't blame them. Cuz is an idiot."

"Hey, he's my friend."

"Is he?" she asked. "Anyway, if he gets everything he wants from his parents, why does he steal so much from shops?"

"'Cause it's cool. Look what I got!" Will, beaming, held up his two new T-shirts.

"*You're* shoplifting, too? Oh, Will."

"I'm just the lookout. But the guys say it's a really important job."

"Dad will flip."

"Dad won't even notice. He doesn't notice

anything these days. Which is lucky 'cause I totally bent my bike during my audacious getaway."

Their conversation, however, was cut short when the computer suddenly and miraculously *ping*ed. Ella and Will looked at the profile page they had created for Henry.

"Oh, my God..." Ella marveled, hardly able to believe it. "We got a message! How is that possible? It's not activated yet."

"Maybe it's a glitch. Maybe they're doing a special free trial. I don't know. But let's not question it. We got a hit! Click on it! Click on it!" Will shouted excitedly.

Ella did. It was their first contact of any kind and they had no idea what to expect. The sender called herself Ms. Truelove, which sounded promising. They couldn't tell what she looked like as her profile picture was from quite far away and her face was obscured under the shadow of a wide-brimmed hat. The children hoped that she didn't have a series of warts in the shape of the Hawaiian Islands on her cheek or something. Regardless, both siblings found her profile page inexplicably comforting. Maybe it was the simple fact that she seemed interested in their father. Maybe it was that she mentioned in her blurb that she liked to give gifts. What-ever it was, Will and Ella immediately liked Ms. Truelove.

"Ask her what type of gifts she likes to give," Will suggested. "We should probably weed out the nuts who don't believe in electronic devices."

"You can't start out by asking about gifts. It'll make Dad sound shallow."

"Why do I feel like you just called me shallow?"

"You *are* shallow."

With that, Ella typed—pretending to be Henry, of course—a brief message back to Ms. Truelove. And, to their joy, a response *ping*ed into their in-box almost immediately. As Ella and Ms. Truelove wrote back and forth, Will excitedly looked over his sister's shoulder offering enthusiastic advice. Some of which Ella took.

"Mention he's a professor…she should know he has a job and isn't a freeloader…

maybe specifically say 'I'm not a freeloader' and 'I own my own house in a very up-and-coming Harlem neighborhood'...tell her..." Will put on a deep voice to imitate Henry. "'I have two adorable scamps....'"

"Scamps?" Ella stopped typing.

"That's how grown-ups talk to each other," Will insisted before resuming his deep voice. "'My son, Will, is particularly handsome and might be a genius.'"

Ella stopped again to look at him, her lips pursed skeptically.

"If you keep stopping," Will complained, "we're never going to finish."

Ella continued typing, including that "my daughter shows some promise as an artist," which is as close as Ella ever got to believing in herself. As the instant messages flew back and forth between Ella's bedroom and wherever it was that Ms. Truelove resided, the two Sullivan siblings were drawn more and more into it. So much so that they didn't hear the garage door open. Nor did they hear Henry's car pull in. Nor did they hear his footsteps on the stairs. Nor did they hear Ella's bedroom door swinging open.

"What are you two doing?!" Henry demanded of his children huddled excitedly over the laptop.

Chapter 6

HENRY STOOD IN the doorway to Ella's pristine room. He had only been listening for 4.3 seconds, but in that brief span of time, he'd heard enough to know what was going on. Will and Ella immediately shrunk back and swallowed.

"It's a school project," Will blurted out, his innate instinct for worming his way out of trouble kicking into overdrive.

Ella looked at him, a little impressed, wondering if this might work.

It wouldn't.

In fact, Henry beat his previous record of 4.3 seconds by figuring out his son was lying in 0.002 seconds, which is faster than a cheetah can blink.

"Let me have that." Henry gestured for Ella's laptop.

She reluctantly handed it to him and he looked at the profile and at the instant message conversation his children had been enjoying with Ms. Truelove. Without saying another word to Will and Ella, he sat down and began typing.

"Dear Ms. Truelove," Henry spoke as he typed. "This is Henry. The *real* Henry. Because, until now, you have been communicating with my twelve-year-old daughter and my fourteen-year-old son, who are now officially grounded until early next year."

Will and Ella simultaneously let out disappointed groans.

"That's unfairly harsh on me," Will said.

"How? It's the same punishment for both of us."

"Yeah, but you don't have any friends, so it won't make any difference to you."

"Shut up! I do have friends." She pushed Will.

"Do not." He pushed her back and Ella fell into her easel, breaking it.

"Look what you did!" Ella shouted at Will.

"You fell into it. Not me."

"Will broke his bike!" shouted Ella to Henry.

Will sharply inhaled in shock at Ella's betrayal. But before he could respond, Henry shouted, "SIT!"

They did.

Henry continued calmly typing and talking. "I appreciate that there are people out there in the world who feel compelled by loneliness and boredom and a general sense of sadness to reach out to total strangers on the internet, in a desperate—pathetic even—search for love in the shape of some kind of mutually beneficial human companionship." He paused. "I am not one of them. I had love. A great love. A once-in-a-lifetime, fireworks-exploding, every-fiber-of-my-being, overwhelming, all-encompassing, rare, and exotic love. I would go on, but it was a love that simply cannot be explained to those who have not experienced it. But that love has ended. It's gone away. Cut short by the cruel whims of the universe...and a series of shameful misdiagnoses that wasted precious months.

"I'm not looking for another love. I would be wasting my time. Having experienced real love, anything else would be a pale, weak, unsatisfactory imitation. Besides, I don't have time to look for love, as all of my spare time is taken up trying to keep my errant children from deceiving vulnerable women on the internet. But I do genuinely wish you all the best in your search for an equally vulnerable man. I'm sure he's out there for you. Exclamation point. Sincerely, Henry." He pressed SEND, handed the laptop back to Ella, and walked downstairs to pour himself a stiff gin and tonic in the last remaining fancy cut glass tumbler that had been part of a set given to him and Katie as a wedding present all those years ago.

Dropping onto the overstuffed sofa and putting his feet up on the coffee table, Henry turned on the TV to a sporting event involving two teams he didn't care about at all. He enjoyed his drink, satisfied in the knowledge that his message to Ms. Truelove would be the end of the whole affair.

On the First Day

Chapter 7

WEATHER-WISE, IT had been one of those grim, gray New York City winters. Rainy and cold, with a biting wind. No snow to beautify or *fun-ify* the otherwise unrelenting bitterness. But no matter how chilly it was outside, it was equally chilly *inside* the Sullivan household the next morning. Will was not talking to Ella, since she had finked on him about the broken bike. Ella wasn't talking to Will because he was responsible for her broken easel. And Henry was doing the *I'm-still-disappointed-in-you* thing that was probably more annoying than when he was just being angry.

The three of them managed to avoid each other all morning, passing in the hallway with

little more than a nodded grunt of acknowl-
edgment. Hunger drove them momentarily
into the kitchen at the same time. Henry
sipped his cheap instant coffee hidden behind
the wall of yesterday's newspaper swiped from
the teacher's lounge. Ella unenthusiastically
stirred her microwave oatmeal, wishing they
had sugar or honey or jam or fruit or *anything* to liven up the gloopy, plain dullness.
But they didn't. They never did. It wasn't "in
the budget," as Henry told them so often
that they had stopped asking. Ella spooned
some oatmeal into her mouth and swallowed
it down just to silence any potential loud
tummy rumblings that might draw unwanted
attention to her later in class. And Will
crunched on plain toast, knowing better than
to look for anything as exotic or delicious as
butter or, God forbid, peanut butter in their
bare cupboards.

A sharp knock on the front door, however,
focused their collective attention.

"Delivery!" a voice shouted from the porch.

The three Sullivans looked at each other
quizzically. A quick survey established that

nobody had ordered anything. And anyone who knew them knew not to send anything for Christmas. So it was with a total sense of mystery that Henry opened the front door a moment later. It was even stranger that, although he had rung the doorbell not thirty seconds ago, the deliveryman and his van had somehow already disappeared. But a midsize wooden crate had been left on the threadbare doormat.

"Truelove Nurseries." Henry read aloud the words stenciled on the crate. He then turned to his children and repeated with emphasis, "*Truelove* Nurseries?"

"Open it, open it," encouraged Will excitedly, missing the point.

"You gave our name and *address* to a stranger on the internet?"

"No, we didn't. I promise," Ella assured her father.

"Oh, so Ms. Truelove just guessed our address and got super lucky?" asked Henry sarcastically.

"*Open* it," repeated Will. "I mean, it's here now so we might as well see what it is."

He crossed his fingers, closed his eyes, and whispered, *"Be an Xbox, be an Xbox, be an Xbox…"*

"The crate is way too big to be an Xbox, Will," an annoyed Ella pointed out.

"Be two Xboxes, be two Xboxes, be two Xboxes…" Will adapted his chant.

Having carried the crate inside the house, Henry rummaged in the hall closet for a hammer and used the back of it to pry open the crate. When the last corner of the panel was loose, he pulled off the front to reveal…

"A *tree*?" Will said, managing to whine *tree* into a three-syllable word.

That is what was inside the crate. A small, chest-height, spindly tree with a dense green bush at the top. In a pot.

"I think it's nice of Ms. Truelove to send a tree," said Ella.

"What are we supposed to do with it?" asked Henry.

"Plant it in the garden?" Ella timidly suggested.

"That's not happening," Henry dismissed.

As they looked at the tree in varying degrees

of disappointment, they were surprised when the dense, leafy bush at the top suddenly rustled.

"The bush moved!" Will pointed.

As if to prove Will right, it moved again.

"Ugh! There's something in there." Ella recoiled.

It was Will and Henry's turn to recoil next when a small beaked and feathered face poked its head out from between the branches. They both fell back, uttering exclamations of surprise.

"A *bird?*" Ella said, giving an involuntary shiver.

"That is literally the opposite of an Xbox," commented Will.

"Do you have any idea how many germs birds carry?" asked Ella.

"You still think your Ms. Truelove is so nice and sweet now, Ella?" asked Henry.

"Well, her *intentions* might have been pure," Ella answered, wanting to believe the best in others.

"Well," Henry decreed, "you invited Ms. Truelove into our lives, so you're responsible for the bird until I can figure out what to do with it."

"Me?" exclaimed Ella while Will laughed.

"No, *you* as in both of you," elucidated Henry, shutting Will up.

With that, Henry picked up his tepid coffee and old newspaper and went upstairs to his room.

Chapter 8

WITH HIS COAT pulled up around his ears and hands jammed firmly into his pockets, Will walked through the cold to the pet shop six blocks away. He would have ridden his bike. But that—through nobody's fault but his own—was not an option. He crossed Morningside Park, passing its waterfall and ornamental pond. There were owners walking dogs, their hands wrapped in plastic bags ready to pounce at the first sign of pooping. There were parents pushing babies in elaborate buggies with cupholders, video screens, and Wi-Fi. There were joggers hooked up to devices that charted their route, their heartbeat, their caloric burn, and their stock portfolio performance in real time.

Will saw none of it. As he came out
the other side of the park and turned onto
Broadway, he could only think about all the
things he'd rather be doing than walking
through the piercing wind to buy whatever it
is that chicks eat. Turns out, they eat insects,
according to the old man who ran the pet
store on the corner of Broadway and 109th
Street.

"You're in luck. I have the correct type of
food right here."

"*So* much luck," Will said sarcastically,
paying for the bag of dead insects and leaving
the store.

As he exited, Will saw Cuz, Bean, Fash,
and Noodle walking toward him. Will's heart
sank. He wanted these guys to think of him
as a cool kid who took risks and didn't care.
Not as someone who buys insects for his pet
bird. He thought about hiding, but it was
too late.

"Yo! Will!" shouted Cuz.

"What're you doing in a pet shop?" asked
Bean disdainfully.

"Oh. Uh." Will thought fast. "The guy lets

me feed mice to the snake. They swallow them whole."

"Whoa, awesome," said Noodle, although no one was quite sure if he thought the awesome bit was watching a snake eat a mouse or the idea of swallowing food whole.

"You're a weird kid, Sullivan," said Fash. "But I like you."

Will let out a sigh of relief. He was beginning to feel like he was definitely one of the gang. But that was all put at risk as a short, pale boy with thick glasses rounded the corner and approached them. This was Benny. He had once been Will's best friend. But that was a long time ago. Before Will's mother died. The last thing he needed was to be greeted by an asthmatic, myopic ex-friend with a bowl haircut and...

"Hi, W-w-w-Will."

...a stutter.

"Who's your friend, *W-w-w-Will*?" joked Cuz. The others snickered.

"Uh...well, he's not a friend," rambled Will. "I hardly know the kid. Our mothers were friends. Years ago. They forced us to play together. You know what mothers are like."

Benny, looking hurt, began to form a word with his lips to say something, but in the pause caused by his stutter, the older boys stepped in.

"Oh, yeah, my parents used to try to make me play with some loser who lived in the same building," said Noodle. "That stopped when I ate his Chinese fighting fish."

Everyone laughed.

"You know what the problem with eating Chinese fighting fish is? You're always hungry again an hour later."

Everyone laughed more, including Will, who actually didn't get why that was funny.

"Hey, kid, what's your name?" Bean asked the boy.

"B-b-b-b-b . . ." He was willing out the word *Benny*.

Will was desperate for him to spit it out, too. But it didn't come fast enough.

"*B-b-b-b-b?*" Bean cut him off. "Your name is *B-b-b-b-b*? What an interesting name."

"How do you do, *B-b-b-b-b?*" Fash bowed.

"Nice to meet you, *B-b-b-b-b*," mocked Cuz.

"It's *Benny*," whispered Will. "His name. It's Benny."

Benny smiled appreciatively at Will, but it didn't last long.

"No, Will," said Fash, "I think you're mistaken. He told us himself. It's B-b-b-b-b."

"Yeah, Will, we say his name is B-b-b-b-b," insisted Noodle. "Or are you telling us we're wrong? Whose side are you on?"

"Yours. Of *course*," said Will.

"Then, what's this kid's name?" Bean asked.

"It's…it's B-b-b-b-b, of course. Good seeing you again, B-b-b-b-b," said Will with a forced laugh. He turned to the four older boys. "I gotta get back home. See you guys later, right?"

Having confirmed that he'd be hanging out with the guys soon, and without looking Benny in the eye again, Will turned his back and marched quickly toward Morningside Park and his home beyond it.

Chapter 9

IF WILL THOUGHT he'd been forced to deal with an uncomfortable situation, he had no idea what his sister, Ella, was going through. With her eyebrows knit together and the corners of her mouth turned down in an exaggerated manner, she stared disdainfully at the chick standing on a piece of newspaper spread out on her bedroom table. Next to it was a shoebox, which was to become his (or her) home once Ella had crafted some kind of nest in it.

She carefully packed the shoebox with construction paper that she had neatly cut up and crumpled to make it springy. Then she put a layer of cotton balls on top of the paper. And then, using her fist as a crushing device, she created a small indentation in the middle of it all.

There. That'll do, she thought to herself. *Home.*

Ella then carefully pulled on a pair of oven mitts and, using kitchen tongs, gingerly lifted up the bewildered chick and placed her (or him) in the new nest. The chick stood there looking up at Ella, who looked down at the chick. A few seconds passed.

"Well, go on," urged Ella. "Settle in. Do what you need to do."

The chick didn't move. It remained still like a statue. Seemingly uncomfortable in its new surroundings.

"I've done what I can, bird. That's your home. It's very soft. Sit down. Relax."

But it didn't. It just stood there. Staring at Ella. And Ella stared back. The two of them were locked in a staring competition, whether the bird knew it or not, until Ella finally blinked and let out a frustrated, guttural grunt.

"Aaaagh. What do you want from me?!" Ella demanded.

The bird said nothing. Of course. Birds can't talk.

"Okay, *okay*," Ella said impatiently as if answering a directive, which there hadn't been.

Ella roughly grabbed a paintbrush, dipped it in water, and dabbed it on the square of green paint in her tray of watercolors. Having executed a quick series of wavy green, watery lines on a clean piece of white paper, she bent the paper and tucked it into the three sides of the shoebox, giving the chick a homey diorama of what looked like grass that might surround his (or her) home in the wild.

"There," said Ella. "Is that better?"

Apparently so. Because the chick now patted down the cotton-ball nest with its little talons before dropping down into it and snuggling its butt deeper into the fluffiness. Ella smiled. And then washed her hands thoroughly with hot water and soap before drying them, liberally applying a hand-sanitizing gel, and then cleaning all surfaces with a disinfectant wipe.

Chapter 10

THAT AFTERNOON, HENRY sat at his computer, stretched his fingers a couple of times, and began typing.

Dear Ms. Truelove, I can only assume that the chick and the tree that you sent were already en route when you read my message. An honest mistake, no doubt. If you would simply supply me with your name and address, I will be happy to return the aforementioned items to you at my earliest convenience. Yours sincerely, Henry Sullivan

P.S. I'm sure your intentions were pure, but I believe I'm not alone in thinking that the gifts you chose are extremely odd things to send to someone who hasn't explicitly said, "What I want for Christmas this year is a tiny, winged companion plus some kind of tall, potted shrub." For the health of your future relationships, I would humbly suggest you explore other, simpler gift options.

Send.

He smiled, satisfied in the knowledge that he had finally put an end to the saga *and* helped this poor, lonely woman in her quest for a poor, lonely man. In doing so, he had earned himself a nice glass of whatever full-bodied Italian red wine he had in the cupboard.

On the Second Day

Chapter 11

It might surprise you to learn that quiet, shy Ella was heavily involved in the school's Christmas musical. It doesn't sound like her thing, does it? The spotlights, singing, showing off, and makeup, along with the strutting around onstage before hundreds of eyes scrutinizing your every move. And you'd be right that it wasn't her thing. So it won't surprise you to learn that she was not onstage but in the background. Or to be more precise, *painting* the background.

Ella had volunteered to design and paint the sets for the Christmas musical, *White Christmas*. After all, she loved painting and she loved musicals. And it was an excellent excuse to spend time away from Will and

Henry during what she called the un-festive season at the Sullivan household.

Ella was making great progress. Not that anyone noticed, of course. In just ten days, the musical would be opening to a packed house of students, teachers, and parents on Christmas Eve. Henry Sullivan, despite knowing that his daughter was involved, would not be among the parents to witness Ella's painted sets. Christmas-themed *events* fell under the same ban as Christmas itself.

While painting, Ella watched Sally Kensington onstage, belting out a tune exactly as she'd been trained by her private voice and performance coaches. She was confidently strutting her stuff, hitting her marks, and feeding off the promise of an auditorium full of adoring fans. Her remarkable blue eyes—the color of sparkling Caribbean waters—positively glowed in the lights.

Sally, at age thirteen, was an old hand at this. She had the sort of self-assured, theatrical cuteness that advertising people love to cast in commercials. She had already appeared in three advertisements in which she feigned wide-eyed and overwhelming delight at a doll that poops candy, candy in the form of jewelry, and cereal that is essentially candy.

But the jewel in Sally's crown was her triumphant appearance on *America's Got Talent.* In truth, she was only on-screen for four seconds in a montage of moderately adept children. But the way Sally talked about it you'd have thought that they had dedicated an entire special episode to her talents. They hadn't. Sally was her own best PR, however, and when she passed, kids whispered in awe, "That's the girl who was on *America's Got Talent.*"

Joining Sally onstage was Gus Gustavson, Thor-like middle-school demigod, with bulging muscles, flowing angelic blond hair, and a magnificent chin that would not have looked out of place on an alp. There was a general consensus among both the students *and* the faculty that Gus was the handsomest and most athletic boy at school. On top of all his other talents and abilities, nature had also blessed Gus Gustavson with the sort of delicate, caressing countertenor singing voice that could raise goose bumps on a marble statue of a deaf Philistine.

Ella watched in admiration, then sighed and went back to painting the *White Christmas* backdrops exactly the way she had designed them: neat and orderly, with clean lines and crisp, if slightly predictable, images.

Working alongside Ella was her friend Suzanne, another background type. But even more background-y, if you can imagine such a thing. Suzanne made Ella look positively chatty. Suzanne wasn't even her name. It was Zhu Yan. But on the first day of school, when asked her name, everyone thought she said Suzanne and she was too shy to correct them. Soon the teachers and administrators at school amended their records, crossing out "Zhu Yan" and replacing it with "Suzanne" until that is what her name officially became.

"No, no, no, no," said Ms. Conti, the drama teacher, seated in the front row. "It's... 'la-la-la-LAAA la-la-LAAA,'" she sang a few notes perfectly, secretly wishing she was onstage instead of these precocious children.

"It's not... 'la-la-LAAAA la-la-LAAA,' which is what you are doing, Sally."

"I am *not*," shot back Sally.

"Oh," said Ms. Conti, slightly taken aback. She should have been used to Sally's confident ways by now, but she was still surprised every time Sally denied missing a note or a cue or a word. Sally lived life under the blissful assumption that everything she did, she did perfectly. And if it wasn't perfect, it was most definitely somebody else's fault.

"I think you'll find," Ms. Conti continued with a moderate amount of trepidation, "that you were slightly sharp during the *crescendo*—"

"And I think *you'll* find that my *crescendo* and my *accelerando* and my *sforzando* were pretty much... *perfetto*."

"It's only a small thing," Ms. Conti tried again, "but maybe you could—"

"May I remind you, Ms. Conti, that during my critically acclaimed *televised* appearance on *America's Got Talent*, I heard the bald judge say—and I quote—'Wow! That's hot.'"

As she said that, several members of the cast

and crew mouthed the words *wow, that's hot* in perfect timing. This was not the first time Sally had told this story.

"Yes, Sally," said Ms. Conti with a sigh, "I am aware of your triumphant appearance on a televised variety show. But even televised stars can sing slightly sharp in rehearsals. That's why we have rehearsals."

There was a deathly silence.

Ella watched Sally in awe and fear, which was exactly how Sally wanted people to watch her. But then, to Ella's horror, Sally's attention fell on Ella. And where Sally looked, others looked, too. Suddenly everyone was looking at Ella, who froze. Suzanne hid.

"You!" Sally shouted.

Ella pointed to herself, questioningly.

"Yes, you. Stop painting so loud! That's what put me off!!"

Painting is a notoriously silent activity, which was one of the things Ella liked most about it. But Ella just swallowed and softly apologized.

"I'm sorry, Sally. I'll paint more quietly from now on."

"Good!" Sally said. "Now, everybody, let's get back to rehearsals. From the top!"

"Excuse me, Sally," said Ms. Conti, asserting her authority. "I am the director and I decide where we go from. Now, everybody…from the top."

For the record, while Sally Kensington was performing on the *America's Got Talent* stage, the bald judge was served a steaming cup of lemon and ginger tea. He took one sip and immediately burned his tongue, causing him to exclaim, "Wow! That's hot!"

Chapter 12

WILL AND ELLA walked home from school in silence. It was only a fifteen-minute journey, but in silence it felt longer. Bundled against the cold, they weaved between oncoming pedestrians as they made their way down 125th Street, which was a mishmash of old and new Harlem.

There were still the characterful old barbershops, delis, repair stores, and laundromats. And there was the venerable Apollo Theater, which dominated 125th Street like an imposing, overdressed old lady. But these old businesses were interspersed with shiny new shops that seemed to pop up regularly overnight. There were organic juice bars, sleek-looking fair-trade coffee shops, a store that sold nothing but hats, another that sold nothing but cheese, and several sushi restaurants.

Throughout, Will walked ahead of Ella.

"There's no point walking a few feet in front of me. People still know I'm your sister."

"That's not why I'm walking ahead of you," lied Will.

"Then why don't you walk next to me?"

"Ugh. God." Will slowed down for Ella to catch up. "If it'll shut you up, I will. Better?"

Ella smiled and gave Will a perfectly timed shove with her shoulder, pushing him— *clank!*—into a lamppost.

"Ow! Hey! Stop that," Will protested. "Don't be such a child."

"I *am* a child. And so are you."

Will let out a sarcastic combination scoff-laugh. "Hardly. I'm almost fifteen."

"In *six months.*"

"Yeah, well, whatever. In some countries I can join the army and get married."

"Where?" Ella asked skeptically.

"I don't know. What do I look like? A geography book?"

Will sped up and walked the rest of the way several steps ahead of Ella, who decided to play a game with herself. They were now walking along the residential streets with rows of houses crowded together. As she passed them, Ella looked in the living room windows and tried to guess what treasures were inside the beautifully wrapped boxes liberally piled beneath Christmas trees.

Under her breath, so that Will couldn't hear, Ella said, *"Polaroid camera...paint box...sparkly rain boots..."*

Ella had no idea that, as Will was passing windows, he was whispering, *"Xbox...iPad...remote-control monster truck... walkie-talkies...nine-inch Bowie knife..."*

There was one box, however, that the siblings were never going to guess the contents of. Not in a million years would they get it right. And that box was the box waiting on the doorstep of their very own house. They saw it as they rounded the corner and trotted up the four creaking, chipped wooden steps to their front porch.

"Another delivery?" Ella said. "Who's it from?"

"I don't know. Only one way to find out,"

replied Will, picking up the box and unlocking the front door.

Inside the house, Will took the box straight into the kitchen, where he grabbed a large, dull chopping knife.

"Shouldn't we wait for Dad?" Ella stopped him.

"It's addressed to 'The Sullivans.' We're Sullivans, aren't we?"

He ran the knife along the seams of the box, crisply slicing open the tape, and almost immediately the cardboard flaps sprung open and two white birds burst out, clattering around the kitchen. The children ducked instinctively as the birds swooped and flapped, knocking over glasses. The birds eventually settled on the large wrought-iron light fixture that was now swinging creakily over the fading wooden kitchen table.

"Dad is going to be pissed," warned Ella, coming out from behind the kitchen island.

"He's gonna be *super* pissed," corrected Will, pointing to the words embossed into the cardboard box: *TRUELOVE AVIARIES.*

Chapter 13

As predicted, Henry was indeed super pissed. He did not need to take a moment to think or compose himself. In fact, he began typing as soon as he sat down, since brutal invective seemed to come quite naturally to him these days.

Dear Ms. Truelove, I thought I had made myself clear in my previous message. Apparently not. So, please forgive my bluntness, but I feel it is necessary in this situation...

I am not interested in a relationship.

Not with you. Not with your attractive, rich, clever sister. Not with Scarlett Johansson. Not with Scarlett Johansson's attractive, rich, clever sister. Not with anyone. Not now. Not soon. Not in the near future. Not after a respectable period of time. Not ever.

Therefore, please stop sending gifts. I assure you they will do nothing to change my mind. Nothing. In fact, if anything, they are having the opposite effect. If anything, they are convincing me that, even if I were in the market for a relationship—which I am not—I would carefully avoid someone who thought that live, feathered creatures and shrubbery make enticing gifts. If anything, it shows a shocking lack of good judgment, which is something a person would need to exhibit in abundance before I would even consider embarking on a relationship with them.

So, to sum up 1) I'm not interested in a relationship with you. 2) I never will be. 3) Your bizarre choice of gifts will do nothing to change my mind. So 4) PLEASE STOP SENDING GIFTS TO US!

Sincerely, Henry Sullivan

He pressed SEND.

"Ella, here's your computer back," he said as he pushed the open laptop across the kitchen table past the large delivery pizza.

Plop!

Bird poop splattered squarely in between the *T* and the *G* keys.

"Ew!" Ella squealed in disgust, looking up at the white birds that were still perched on the light fixture above them. They cooed nonchalantly...like it's no big deal to poop on the keyboard of someone else's computer. Let me tell you, it *is* a big deal to poop on the keyboard of someone else's computer. You absolutely should not do that. It is very much frowned upon.

Will laughed as Ella tore several paper towels and attempted to skillfully remove the poop without spreading it. No easy task, especially while wearing ski gloves. They were all wearing gloves. And thick coats and woolly hats. Why? Because it was freezing outside and the windows had been wide-open all afternoon in an attempt to lure the birds out of the house. But no amount of coaxing, encouraging, or newspaper waving could convince the birds to take advantage of the open windows.

In fact, the birds were very possibly the only ones in the room who wouldn't have preferred to be somewhere else.

On the Third Day

Chapter 14

THAT MORNING, AS he showered, Henry knew
he had to concentrate on making things right
with Dean Grumpf. The guy was a conceited
name-dropper and a poor academic, but fate
had made him Henry's boss. And the truth
was, Henry could not afford to lose his job.
Their big old house was expensive to main-
tain. And so were his children, who, rather
inconsiderately, kept growing, requiring new
clothing at an alarming rate.

As a sought-after caterer and chef, Katie had
contributed greatly to their finances...and to
Henry's waistline. She managed to cook all
day for other people and, then, still amaze
the family with a sumptuous supper that they
would all enjoy together, delighting at four-

year-old Ella's determined attempts to get a forkful of peas from the plate to her mouth before they all ended up on the floor.

But now, even after economizing and belt tightening, it was a stretch for Henry to cover the shortfall. While his expenses had only gone up over the past five years, his salary had not.

It was a new day, and he would have to be a new Henry. A calculating Henry, who could convincingly pretend to like Dean Grumpf's book and even like Dean Grumpf himself.

Katie used to tease Henry by telling him in a mock-serious voice, "Sincerity—once you can fake that, you got it made." She then always added a sincere-sounding compliment, like "Have you lost weight?" knowing full well that Henry definitely had *not* lost weight.

Glad that the saga with Ms. Truelove was now well and truly behind them, Henry committed 100 percent of his time and attention to saving his job. That, he decided, was the best and most responsible thing he could do for himself and for his family.

When he had rinsed the last of the soap off

his legs and watched it swirl down the drain, Henry turned off the shower and, in the quiet, could finally hear his daughter shouting.

"Dad!...*Dad!*...DAD!"

Throwing on a frayed bathrobe his wife had surprised him with while they were dating, Henry trudged into Ella's room.

"What?!" he asked, squeezing water from the ends of his beard.

"Look," she said ominously, pointing out her window at the dark, overgrown garden behind the house.

Henry looked skeptical. Nothing should be in there. He'd made sure of that five years ago when he slapped a padlock on the gate that led from the garden to the side street and bolted the back door of the house.

But there *was* something in there.

"Is that...a chicken?" Henry whispered.

"Look closer," instructed Ella.

"*Two* chickens!!" Henry corrected himself.

"Keep looking," Ella encouraged.

"Wait...*THREE* chickens???!! What are three chickens doing in the garden?!" Henry's mind immediately went to the most likely source of tomfoolery in their house. "Will! WILL!" Henry shouted.

"What?" Will answered, entering Ella's room with a toothbrush sticking out of his foamy mouth.

"Do you know anything about the chickens in the garden?"

"The *what* in the *where*?"

Seeing that Will truly had no idea what he was talking about, Henry concluded that one of the neighbors must be responsible.

Followed by Will and Ella, Henry marched downstairs to the back door, where he paused for a moment, staring at the locks on the door separating the house from the garden. He took a deep breath, seized the bolt, and struggled to pull it open. Five years without movement had made it stick. Eventually, it gave way and slid across with a *thunk*. Henry opened the door and they were immediately greeted by a gust of cold air as they stepped over a slithery tangle of intertwining roots, weeds, and foliage.

This was the first time any of them had set foot in the garden in five years. Once it had been a playground, a picnic area, a vegetable farm, and a fruit grove. Now the garden was dark and foreboding. To Will and Ella, it seemed larger than they remembered. To Henry, it felt claustrophobic.

The garden was surrounded on each side by a neighboring house, and Henry was in long-running disputes with the owners of all three. One had a dog whose favorite poop spot was directly beside the Sullivans' front porch. Another cooked with far too many strong spices, the smells of which wafted straight into Henry's bedroom. And the third played their opera music far too loud on summer evenings (although some would say that playing opera even very softly was still too loud).

"Who did this?!" Henry shouted, pivoting his gaze between his three neighbors' houses. "Hm?! Was it you, Mr. Greenblatt? Just because I might have flung your dog's poop back into your yard? I see you there, twitching the curtain…and you, too, Mrs. Poku. I see you. Did you drop chickens in here? Just because I don't like opera blasting at all hours and might have reported you to noise pollution a couple times? Is this your payback? Is it?"

"Dad." Ella tugged at his bathrobe. *"Da-ad."*

"Don't interrupt. I am trying to get to the bottom of this."

"Dad," Will said sharply, backing up Ella. "Look."

Henry looked where Will pointed. There was a metal tag attached to the left claw of each chicken. Henry bent down, squinted at the letters embossed on the tags, and after a moment, to his horror, made out the words *TRUELOVE FARMS.*

Chapter 15

HENRY'S FINGERS purposefully punched the keys on his laptop as he composed yet another email to Ms. Truelove.

> Listen, Truelove, I've pretty much had it with your shenanigans. I don't know if you think you're being funny or something, but let me tell you: you are not. You are not funny or charming or intriguing or playful or endearing. You are, in fact, annoying, obtuse, misguided, and annoying. Yes, I know I wrote "annoying" twice. I left it that way for a reason: You are being double annoying!

Chickens? Really? Chickens. Not just one. Three. And that's on top of the two pooping birds yesterday and the chick in the tree two days ago. None of these gifts is appropriate.

There is a common sporting expression, "three strikes and you're out." Well, Ms. Truelove, over the past three days, you've had your three strikes. You are out.

One more gift—I'm warning you—and there will be trouble.

Sincerely, Henry Sullivan

SEND.

Henry sat back in his chair. Mission surely accomplished.

And then he heard the doorbell ring.

Chapter 16

"DON'T ANSWER IT! I got it!" Henry shouted as he ran down the stairs, two at a time.

Will and Ella watched as the panting Henry grabbed the handle and swung the door open.

"No, thank you, we don't want it!" he said before even seeing who was standing there.

"Want what?" asked a woman in her thirties, wearing an official-looking khaki uniform with a badge on it.

"Whatever it is you're delivering. We don't want it."

"I'm not a delivery person," the woman said mildly indignantly before explaining, "I'm from Animal Protection Services." She tapped her chest badge emblazoned with a rotund panda gnawing on a bamboo shoot and encircled by small golden birds that looked a bit like stars.

"Oh," said Henry.

"Aren't you going to apologize, Dad?" asked Ella, peering at the woman from behind Henry.

"What for?"

"No need," said the woman with a smile. She had a faintly Hispanic accent. "I'm sure it was an honest mistake."

"Exactly," said Henry. "See? No need to apologize. She just said so." Henry turned his attention back to the woman and impatiently asked, "Well? What can I do for you?"

"You can pay this fine," she said as she handed him a piece of paper.

"Fine?! What for?!" Henry objected.

"For keeping agricultural fowl on a residential street without appropriate housing or adequate facilities."

"Fowl? What fowl? I don't know what you're talking about," Henry lied.

"I think she's talking about the three chickens in the garden," said Will, who was quite enjoying his father's discomfort.

"Thank you for explaining," said Henry sarcastically.

"Hens, actually," the woman said. "They're hens."

"How could you possibly know what we have in our private garden that cannot be seen from the street?" Henry asked suspiciously.

"Oh…one of your neighbors might have, you know…"

"Turned us in? Narc'ed on us?" Will offered.

"Precisely." She nodded.

"Look, Ms. …" Henry started.

"Mariana," she lilted, clipping the *r* musically. "You can call me Mariana."

"Listen, Mariana, these chickens—"

"Hens," corrected Ella.

"These *hens* are not our birds. We don't even like birds. Seriously. They're pests. It's like fining us for having ants or rats or termites. We do not like or want birds in our house."

At that moment, there was a delicate *plop plop* and two perfectly round white poops landed squarely on the paper fine that Henry was holding. Any hope of convincing Mariana that the Sullivans did not collect birds went out the window…unlike the birds themselves, who still *refused* to go out the window. Mariana looked up at the small white birds perched on the entrance hall light fixture above them.

"You have a lot of birds for people who don't like birds," Mariana said before looking again, more closely, at the birds. "Wait. Do you have…*Streptopelia turtur?*"

"Is that a disease?" panicked Ella, her throat beginning to feel scratchy. "I knew it. I *knew* it. Filthy birds! Am I blotchy?"

"No, the *birds* are *Streptopelia turtur.* It's a type of dove," explained Mariana. "Totally harmless. But very rare and very protected…I don't suppose you have a legally required import license for them, do you?"

They did not. And Mariana handed Henry a second—much heftier—fine, silently mouthing the word *sorry* as she did so.

Chapter 17

ENOUGH WAS ENOUGH for Henry as he gripped the steering wheel of his nine-year-old Volvo SUV and pointed it north on I-87 out of the city. Harlem and then the Bronx became dots in his rearview mirror, giving way to greenery (and brownery and some blue-ery when they passed a reservoir). Not that Will and Ella, in the back seat, could see much through the darkness.

It was 1:15 a.m. and the Sullivan family were on a mission...a mission that Will and Ella would gladly have missed in order to stay tucked up in bed. But, as Henry told them, "You got us into this Ms. Truelove–shaped mess. You can help get us out of it."

The code name for the mission—if

they had come up with one, which they hadn't—could have been *Operation Fowl Play* or *Operation Fly Away* or *Operation Abandon-the-birds-in-a-remote-location-and-drive-away-at-great-speed*. The two white doves were in a large box in the back of the SUV along with the three hens, while the partridge chick was sitting on Will's lap eating freeze-dried mealworms from his palm.

"That's disgusting," groaned Ella. "Do you have any idea how unhygienic that is?"

"You want one?" He held a dried worm up in Ella's face.

"Ew! Get it away from me." She slapped his hand away, knocking the dead worm to the floor.

"Knock it off," Henry said over his shoulder. "We're here."

He left the paved road, steering onto a darkened dirt path. He carried on for a while until he finally applied the brakes and turned off the engine by a copse of large oak trees.

Ella and Will looked out the window. It was quiet. And dark. Really quiet and dark. It was incredible that you can be somewhere so dark and quiet just an hour from the city, which was permanently so lit and loud. But it was a cloudy night so the moon and stars were obscured by a layer of gray. With the engine off, they could only hear the soft whistling of the wind blowing around their car.

"If I was a werewolf hungry for the flesh of twelve-year-old girls, this is exactly the sort of place I'd hang out," said Will to Ella, who tried not to show how scared she was by the thought of that.

"You're right, Will," said Henry.

"Dad?!" exclaimed Ella, betraying the fear she was trying to hide.

"No, Ella, he's right...which is why *he* should get out of the car and let the birds go instead of us."

"What?!" shouted Will in a similar pitch to Ella.

"Yeah," agreed Ella, "everyone knows that werewolves avoid stinky fourteen-year-old boys...usually. So you get the honor of going out into the dark and the cold to release the birds."

"Why don't *you?*" Will asked of his father.

"Somebody has to stay here with Ella in case the werewolves make an appearance." Henry smiled. "Go on, Will. Out," he urged before turning to Ella, while opening a bag he'd brought with him. "Cookie?"

"Don't mind if I do," replied Ella. "And, Will…don't leave the door open. It's cold outside."

Will groaned and exited the car. Henry had thoughtfully left the car lights on so that Will could see what he was doing and wouldn't trip over a tree stump, impaling himself on a sharp branch or anything. Will opened the trunk of the car and shooed the hens out. They jumped down to the ground with a flightless flutter of their wings. He then reached in for the box with the pair of white birds. He opened the top and they just sat there.

"Go on," he encouraged. "Be free."

With that, he gave the box a little shake and the two birds flew out, but only as far as the closest branch, from where they continued to watch Will. The only one left was the little partridge, who Will had placed on top of the car while he dealt with the other birds. Will picked it up and looked at his (or her) face made red by the color cast from the brake lights at the back of the car.

"All right, Alan." Which is what Will had randomly named the little bird. "It was sort of nice to meet you. But I think the Ward Pound Ridge Reservation is a better place for you than a residential street in Harlem."

He carefully placed the partridge in the long grass at the base of a large tree and turned to leave, stopping himself after a step and turning back.

"Nearly forgot. You probably need these more than I do." He poured the remainder of the freeze-dried mealworms onto the grass for Alan. But then Will took a pinch of worms back and snuck them into his pocket, thinking it might be hilarious to leave a few under Ella's pillow.

Will jumped back into the warmth of the car, closing the door quickly after him, and Henry began the drive back to town. Will was pleasantly surprised that Ella had kept a cookie for him. As he ate it, he thought better of his mealworms-under-the-pillow prank and buzzed down the window briefly to scatter the freeze-dried invertebrates to the outside world.

Henry then surprised his children by stopping at a twenty-four-hour drive-through fast-food restaurant and treating them to burgers, fries, and milkshakes. It might have been the first time they'd been out for dinner all together in five years.

They drove back in silence, except for the chewing and slurping of their meals and the catchy musical musings of Taylor Swift, who, remarkably, satisfied the listening tastes of all three Sullivans.

By the time they arrived home and pulled into the garage, Will and Ella were virtually sleepwalking. Henry ushered them gently into the house, telling them to go straight upstairs to bed. It reminded Henry, for a moment, of when they used to take family road trips and he and Katie would have to carry the two sleeping children up to bed. But when they arrived in the living room, they all stopped. Shocked into stillness. Unable to move. And all quite wide-awake again.

For there in the living room, they were greeted by the sight of the three hens... and the two white birds... and the chick. All nonchalantly milling about like nothing had happened.

On the Fourth Day

Chapter 18

NONE OF THE Sullivans had a good night's sleep. How could they? Each of them was entirely freaked out by the reappearance of the birds. There was no denying it. It was super freaky to find the birds—which they had just deposited over an hour outside the city—waiting for them inside their house. More than just *freaky*, it was impossible. And yet it had happened.

They each spent the night tossing and turning, trying to make logical sense of it. Angry accusations had been thrown back and forth between them at three o'clock in the morning. Had Will simply *not* put the birds out and they'd come home in the back of the car? Did the birds have some kind of homing instinct that brought them immediately back to this house? Did they follow the trail of the mealworms that Will sprinkled carelessly from the car on the drive home? And if so, had Ella or Henry left a window or the front door open for them to reenter the house on their own?

In brief, whatever element of closeness that had begun to creep into their relationship during *Operation That-didn't-work-out-very-well-did-it* evaporated into a melee of shouting and finger pointing before bed.

Henry had only just finally fallen into a decent sleep when he had the rug of slumber cruelly whipped out from under him.

"SQUAWK! SQUAWK SQUAWK!!! SQUAWK SQUAWK!!!"

Henry sat bolt upright, his heartbeat racing. Some animal was calling out in the loudest, most annoying tone ever devised. Henry attempted to shrug on his bathrobe while clasping his hands over his ears. He looked out of his bedroom window for the source of the appalling noise. Lights flicked on in his neighbors' windows, too, as they tried to do the same. Seeing each other, they opened their windows and shouted.

"What is that?!" Henry shouted to Mrs. Poku. "Some new form of experimental opera?!"

"No, it's not me," she shouted angrily, while closing up the top of her dressing gown, for which Henry was grateful. "It sounds like it's coming from *your* house."

"Well, it's absolutely not me!" Henry responded.

Mr. Greenblatt's window opened and his bald head appeared. "Henry! Look on your front porch. That's where the noise is coming from!" Greenblatt shouted.

Oh, no, thought Henry. *It can't be.*

But it was.

Henry opened his front door and on the doorstep was a large, elaborate birdcage. A vast architectural masterpiece of scrolling, twisting iron in the shape of a Gothic-revival palace. And within its bars were four birds with jet-black feathers and yellow eyes, squawking ceaselessly with all their might at earsplitting decibels.

Will and Henry carried the birdcage into the house, where Ella had the good sense to throw a blanket over it. The birds were immediately convinced that once again it was nighttime and ceased their calling. The three relieved Sullivans dropped simultaneously into the sofa, from where they could all see the manufacturer's label on the birdcage and from where they could all experience the same sinking feeling in the pit of their stomachs.

The manufacturer was TRUELOVE IRON-WORKS.

Chapter 19

"I GOT IT! It's so simple," said Will, who was by far the most cunning of the three. At least, he certainly thought he was. "We just google *Truelove Ironworks,* find out where they are, go there, and confront Ms. Truelove."

They all agreed that was actually an excellent idea.

But Will had a hidden motive that Ella suspected. Clearly this Ms. Truelove was some kind of wealthy industrialist with the means to supply extravagant (if misguided) gifts to those she liked. Will was secretly hoping that Henry would get face-to-face with her and fall hopelessly in love at first sight. Once they were in love, Will would be able to work his charm on Ms. Truelove to nudge her expensive-gift-giving instincts away from wildfowl and toward, say, gaming-related electronics.

Will was as cunning as a fox...who had earned a dual PhD in Guile and Trickery...from the University of Slyness.

But it turns out Ms. Truelove might have had a *triple* degree from the University of One-Step-Ahead-of-You because, no matter how much they surfed or how deep they dived into the internet, the Sullivans could not find any mention of Truelove Ironworks. Not in New York State, nor the whole East Coast, nor the entirety of the United States and its protectorates and provinces. Nothing!

They then tried searching for Truelove Farms. Nada.

Truelove Nurseries. Bubkes.

Truelove Aviaries? Squat.

Letting out a deep sigh, Henry knew they needed help.

Chapter 20

"WE NEED HELP!" Henry shouted.

"OH! OKAY! SURE!" Mariana, the animal protection lady, shouted back over the squawking of the black birds in their ornate cage. She dropped the cloth back down, silencing them once again.

Mariana sat down in an oversize armchair. She was petite. *Petite* is French for *small*. But when you call someone small, it can sound like an insult. For some reason saying it in French makes it more of a compliment. So... Mariana was petite.

She had a quiet air of confidence. And, as she spoke, her faint accent conjured thoughts of tropical breezes over warm South American waters. When she smiled, which was

107

often, her bright hazel eyes displayed a corona of crow's-feet at the corners. Her olive skin radiated a healthy glow, which was the result of a childhood spent outdoors in the sun playing with lizards, riding horses, and swimming in nature. Her nose was delicate and pointed, with a slight kink, like someone had gently stubbed it into the middle of her face. And her sensible-length dark-brown hair was neatly pulled back into a practical ponytail. Mariana's most noticeable feature, however, was her smile, which was expansive and revealed a small but particularly charming gap between her front teeth.

These imperfections—the crow's-feet, the nose kink, the tooth gap—on their own might have looked a bit odd, but they somehow created a very pretty, very interesting, and altogether harmonious picture.

Ella handed her a mug of hot coffee, for which Mariana thanked her and smiled, flashing the mesmerizing tooth gap again.

"Milk?" Ella asked, holding out a bowl of white powder with a spoon in it.

"Surely that's sugar," said Mariana, sweetly

making the first syllable of *sugar* sound like footwear. "*Shoe*-gar."

"No," said Will flatly. "That's milk. Or, at least, a dried milk product."

Mariana tried not to look judgmental but failed.

"It lasts longer than regular milk and doesn't require refrigeration," justified Henry as a chicken flapped into his lap. "Look, we didn't ask you to come here to debate the comparative merits of various dairy products." He sighed and placed the chicken back onto the floor.

"Yes, why *did* you ask me to come?"

"We need you to take the birds," said Will.

"Take them? Where?"

"*Anywhere,*" replied Ella.

"Like an animal shelter?" Henry offered helpfully. The chicken was back on his lap. He brushed it once again onto the floor.

"You don't want them?"

"It's not that we don't want them, Mariana," Ella explained. "It's just that we don't want whatever ticks or bugs or parasites they may be carrying. Ones that might, for example, dig down through your skin and anchor into your flesh so you can't pull them out while they drain you of your blood. Or that might sneak in through your ear canal and lay eggs in your brain. Or deposit some kind of bacteria that creates a flaky red-and-white rash all over your face and body. Y' know, that kind of thing."

Mariana stared at Ella, not quite sure how to respond. She finally decided to simply ask, "Then why did you get them?"

"WILL YOU PLEASE GET OFF ME!" Henry shouted, shaking the chicken from the top of his head, where it had somehow landed. He regained composure and explained, "We didn't get them. They were sent to us."

"All of them?"

"Yes," all the Sullivans said in unison.

"By who?" Mariana asked, scrunching up her face in a way that made her nose look particularly small and pointy.

"We don't know," replied Ella unenthusiastically.

"Someone you don't know sent you four colly birds?" Mariana said, pointing to the huge iron birdcage covered by a blanket.

Ella looked at Mariana curiously and asked, "*What* sort of birds are they?"

"Well," Mariana explained, "they're actually a type of blackbird, but they're referred to as colly birds—because they're black like coal—or sometimes known as *calling* birds because they, as you know, call out a lot."

The Sullivans looked at each other as a curious thought simultaneously began to form in each of their minds independently.

"So," Will said tentatively, "we have been sent four *calling* birds...?"

"And the hens, Mariana," asked Ella in a worried voice, "are they a particular *type* of hen?"

"Yes. Faverolles, I believe," Mariana informed them.

"*Faverolles?* That sounds...French," Will said with a sigh.

"Yes. Very good. They are French hens. How did you know?"

"Lucky guess," he replied as their worrying thought solidified.

"I don't suppose," started Henry, "that those doves you told us we have are actually...

111

turtle doves…" Henry pointed up to the top of the bookcase where the two white birds cooed softly.

"Wow! You guys really know your stuff."

"And a partridge," said Ella, pointing to Alan in his shoebox home.

"…who arrived in—what I'm now assuming was—a…pear tree," Henry whispered hoarsely.

Chapter 21

THE SULLIVANS WERE entirely still like stat-
ues while each internalized the fact that Ms.
Truelove had so far sent them the gifts from
the first four days of the Christmas carol "The
Twelve Days of Christmas." As impossible as
it seemed, the facts were as clear as day.

The Sullivans knew the song well. In fact,
years ago Katie had led them all in multiple
renditions of it while driving home from
her parents' house in Pennsylvania. They had
celebrated Thanksgiving the previous day, and
Henry had protested that November was too
early in the year to be singing carols. But
Katie had insisted that the day after Thanksgiving was, in fact, the official beginning of
the Christmas season, and thus Henry was

obliged to sing. As happened with most of their disagreements, Katie's logic won the day and Henry added his voice to the noisy chorus.

Mariana, unfamiliar with English-language Christmas carols, wondered why they had all gone so eerily quiet.

"It can't be," said Ella finally.

"It is," responded Will. "Holy crap, it *is!*"

"It is what?" Mariana asked, slightly bemused.

"There's a song..." Will began explaining before he was cut off by Henry, who saw no reason to discuss their personal family matters with an outsider. If they started talking about the gifts, they'd have to explain Ms. Truelove, and therefore the dating website and then get into a whole explanation about why Will and Ella felt that they needed to find a wife for their father. It was embarrassing and personal and none of anybody's business but theirs. Besides...it sounded absolutely, positively, 100 percent insane.

"Look. It doesn't matter how we got them. Or who sent them. Just...Mariana, can you take the birds or not?"

"Not," said Mariana, somehow managing to sound both definitive and apologetic at the same time. She went on to explain. "Look, the run-up to Christmas is the busiest time of year for all shelters. They're overworked already. Things slow down in January. Maybe someone can take your birds then."

"January?!" Ella exclaimed, shuddering at the thought of the prolonged exposure to germs.

"Could we just…" Will had another good idea. "…*eat* them?"

"No!" everyone said, emphatically.

"Well, we can't have them just wandering around the place for a month!" Henry pointed out. All three French hens were now sitting at his feet and staring, as if planning how to climb back up and settle on him.

"You certainly *cannot,* Mr. Sullivan."

"So you'll take them?" Henry suddenly became hopeful.

"No. I meant you cannot have them wandering around the place. You need appropriate shelters, adequate bedding, automatic watering facilities…"

"And where are we supposed to get all that?" Henry exclaimed.

"At one of the larger home stores," Mariana said.

There was silence. She looked at the dejected, confused, upset faces around her and quietly offered, "I could...go with you if you want help."

"Yes, please," said Ella almost immediately.

"And then I can show you how to look after them, too," she suggested.

"That would be very helpful," said Will. "Wouldn't it, Dad?"

"Yes, I suppose," said Henry begrudgingly, already annoyed by the time and money that this task would take. He had already begrudgingly paid the fines with hard-earned money that was not budgeted for the care of strange animals. "Right. Get your coats, kids."

As they disappeared, Henry was left alone momentarily with Mariana. The two stood there in silence. It had been a long time since Henry had found himself in a position to converse with a woman who wasn't a student, a colleague, a doctor, a sales assistant, a waitress, a policewoman, or a voice that came onto the phone after he repeatedly shouted *"Rep-re-SEN-ta-tive!"* into an ironically named help line. Rocking back and forth on his feet a little, Henry drew his lips into something approximating a smile.

"The powdered milk," he finally said, pointing to her half-empty coffee mug. "Not so bad, is it?"

"Not bad at all," Mariana lied.

After a pause Henry asked, "You, uh, from New York?"

"No. From Guatemala."

"Oh. Your English is excellent," complimented Henry.

"My parents emigrated to Texas when I was five."

"Oh...do you remember much of the journey? I hear it can be tough. Especially for a kid. Was it?"

"Not especially. We flew first class. My father was senior vice president of Latin American operations for a major conglomeration."

"Ah," said Henry, not at his most eloquent.

"We lived in Austin two years before

returning home, but I picked up the language pretty well. I've only actually been back in America since I got this job six months ago."

"Nice," said Henry, trying to remember how polite small talk worked. Luckily, he was rescued from his awkwardness when his phone rang.

"Hello?" Henry answered, holding one finger up in the air to Mariana, indicating the universal symbol for *hold on one moment, please, don't go anywhere, I just need to answer my phone.*

"Where the hell are you, Henry?" boomed a voice from the other end of the line. "You were supposed to be here ten minutes ago!"

"Hastie!" Henry had forgotten today was his disciplinary peer review. Henry stumbled for an excuse, "Ella fell and…cracked her head open. Blood everywhere. Had to clean it up…no, no. Better now. I'm on my way."

Henry quickly kicked his slippers into the air and shoved his feet into the hall closet, from which they emerged clad in loafers. Grabbing a coat, he turned to Mariana.

"Here." He thrust a credit card and his car

keys into her hand. "Buy whatever you need to buy. Take Will and Ella." The two had arrived back with their coats and shoes on.

"But, Mr. Sullivan," said Mariana incredulously, "you hardly know me."

"Yes. You're right. Of course." He plucked the credit card from Mariana's hand and passed it to Ella. "*You're* in charge of this. Okay. Godspeed. I gotta go. Car's in the garage. Bye…*behave!*" he said, turning to Will and Ella. Mainly Will.

With that stern directive, Henry ran out the door and down the street toward the university campus, grappling with his coat and tying his tie as he went.

Chapter 22

"Good Lord!" exclaimed Provost Fringe when he saw Henry, out of breath, burst into the meeting room in Columbia University's Hamilton Hall. Fringe had been waiting there with an increasingly impatient Dean Grumpf. "Are you wearing two different shoes?"

"Huh?" puffed Henry, looking down and realizing that he was indeed wearing one black shoe and one brown. Not only that, but his tie was off to the side, his hair was mussed from the French hen trying to nest on it, and sweat dripped down his face from the run. "Sorry I'm late, Dean," he said, shaking Dean Grumpf's hand, which felt like a cold, damp jellyfish in his palm.

"Hello, Professor Sullivan," grimaced Dean

Grumpf. The dean was a thin, pale man who always looked like he was sniffing something unpleasant. But in this instance, he actually was. "Why do you smell like…chickens?"

"Chickens? Me?…Oh," replied Henry with a forced, exaggerated laugh, "it must be my new aftershave. It's new. Just got it."

"Eau de *chicken*?" Dean Grumpf asked condescendingly.

"Yeah! I love the smell of farms. Don't you? The great outdoors, nature," Henry babbled mindlessly. "You can get all types of scents these days. You know, there's a bookstore in Florence that sells incense that smells like old books—"

"Why don't we sit down, everyone, and take a breath," said Provost Fringe, stepping in to curtail Henry's rant. "We all know why we're here."

"Yes," agreed Dean Grumpf, "because Professor Sullivan denigrated my scholarly treatise in front of his class."

"*Denigrate* is a strong word," said Provost Fringe.

"And accurate, according to my sources,"

replied Grumpf. "Professor Sullivan described my work using the words—and I quote—*piffle, tripe, baloney,* and *risible.* Do you deny that, Professor Sullivan?"

Henry opened his mouth to issue a firm denial, but Dean Grumpf stopped him. "Before you say anything, Professor, I should tell you I have it all recorded on an audio file."

Henry quickly changed tack. "Firstly, Dean Grumpf, I can see how those words might be interpreted as negative, but personally…I love both tripe and baloney. A baloney sandwich is the greatest, most American of lunchtime treats. And tripe? The edible lining of a farm animal's stomach? What's not delicious about *that*? And, as for *risible,* well, that comes from the Latin *ridere,* which is 'to laugh,' and who doesn't love to laugh? So, you see, it really is a big misunderstanding."

Henry looked at the faces of Grumpf and Fringe. Neither seemed convinced. With a lofty gaze from his glassy, fishlike eyes, Grumpf merely continued to list Henry's indiscretions.

"My sources also tell me that Professor

Sullivan is regularly ten minutes late for his classes and often lets the class out ten minutes early, which deprives his students of *one-third* of the class time that they have paid for."

"Yes, w-well, m-maybe, occasionally I—" Henry stammered, but he was cut off by Dean Grumpf, who was on a roll.

"My sources also suspect that Professor Sullivan doesn't actually read their papers but instead assigns random grades with arbitrary notes."

"Now, hang on a minute," said Henry, sounding indignant, "that's entirely unfair."

"Provost," Grumpf turned to Fringe and held up three exam papers. "I have here three exam papers in which the students cut and pasted in one full page of *Alice in Wonderland*, which seems to have gone entirely unnoticed."

"What grade did I give them?" Henry asked.

"C plus."

"Exactly. Without the *Alice in Wonderland*, it would've been a B."

Provost Fringe rubbed his eyes as Dean Grumpf pulled out a small pad, flicked to a certain page, and continued to list Henry's offenses, including canceling office hours, falling asleep during class, eating sandwiches while lecturing, teaching the wrong class, appearing mildly inebriated, appearing quite inebriated, not updating course material, appearing *very* inebriated, and stealing sandwiches from the communal fridge in the professors' lounge.

"I don't think you take your academic responsibilities seriously, Professor Sullivan. In fact, some might say that these transgressions are grounds for dismissal. Especially jealously attacking a colleague's groundbreaking academic work."

"Jealous?!" exclaimed Henry, incensed that someone might think him envious of Grumpf's middling intellect.

"Okay, okay…Dean Grumpf," interjected Provost Fringe, "I understand what your concerns are, but surely talk of dismissal is premature. Yes, Professor Sullivan seems to struggle *at times* with certain professorial standards. But it should also be mentioned that his lectures are also very often impassioned and insightful. And his class is still one of the most popular and oversubscribed in your department."

While Dean Grumpf ruminated on this, Provost Fringe continued, "And, as for his so-called attack on your most excellent book, I can tell you he didn't mean anything by it. In fact—if I remember correctly—he told me that he was simply demonstrating to his class how brilliant works, such as your own, can be taken out of context and twisted into lies, which is a valuable academic lesson for future leaders and academics. Don't you agree?"

Dean Grumpf looked at Henry, then said, "Is *that* what you were doing?"

"Yes. Exactly. That." Henry nodded vigorously. "What he just said. And, honestly, your book is…extremely…" Henry searched desperately for the words. "…well put together. Yeah. The binding is solid. The pages follow one another in a perfect sequential order. The…cover art is arresting. I love the font. Strong, yet delicate. It's exceedingly well punctuated. And…makes some bold conclusions and claims that…most academics…would, uh, never—really, *never*—put their name to.

So, um, I stand in awe of you for, y' know, having the courage to put it all out there the way you did."

Dean Grumpf's face still wore the expression of someone who had just swallowed a rancid oyster. But that, believe it or not, was an improvement compared to his usual pinched expression. He was clearly softening.

"And let's not forget the tragedy that Professor Sullivan has suffered," continued Provost Fringe, driving home the point. "To lose a wife. That must account for a lot of these... *eccentricities,* which can be attributed to a still-fragile mental and emotional state. I think maybe he's still in that phase. At the *end* of that phase, though. The *very end.*" Fringe looked pointedly at Henry. "Am I right, Professor Sullivan?"

Henry did not like to use Katie's death as an excuse, but he could tell his friend, Hastie, knew what he was doing. Henry sighed.

"Yes. The end of that stage."

"Hm. I suppose," conceded Dean Grumpf, adding, "you are clearly still emotionally and mentally impaired from that. And I do appreciate your recognition of my bravery in writing a… is that a *bird* in your pocket?"

Henry looked down at his coat pocket. There, indeed, the partridge chick was looking up at him. If beaks could smile, Henry would have sworn it was smiling at him. The damned thing must have climbed into his coat pocket for warmth while the coat was strewn over the back of the sofa. Having been in such a hurry, Henry hadn't noticed when he grabbed it and swung it on.

"No," Henry said, rapidly pushing the chick's head back down.

"Yes, it was," corrected Dean Grumpf. "You have a *bird* in your pocket."

At that moment, the partridge chick actually jumped out of Henry's pocket and landed lightly on the ground. All three men watched, mesmerized, as it waddled straight over to Dean Grumpf.

"If I may ask… *why* are you carrying a bird in your pocket?" Grumpf asked.

Provost Fringe held his breath, hoping that Henry had a good answer. Carrying around a bird in your pocket hardly makes you look *more* sane and rational, which had been his goal for Henry throughout this meeting. Knowing this, Henry could hardly admit that this partridge was one of ten birds that had arrived on his doorstep over the past four days, sent by a mysterious internet stalker.

"Uhhhhhh, it's my…emotional support animal," replied Henry.

"Your *emotional support animal*?" Dean Grumpf repeated, smirking at Fringe as if to say, *is this the type of professor you want teaching your students?*

The little partridge chick then hopped up on Dean Grumpf's shoe and picked its way up the dean's outstretched leg, past his lap, onto his arm, and up to his shoulder, where the partridge stood, staring blankly, eye to eye, with the dean.

"Hello, little fella, do you look after Professor Sullivan? Are you his confidant? His sober buddy?" Grumpf chuckled to himself. "Maybe *you* should be teaching a class at…*AAAAaaaaGGGGGggghhhhhh!!!*"

That is not how Dean Grumpf had intended to finish the sentence. He had intended to say, "at Columbia University," which would have made a lot more sense. But, instead, he shouted, "at *AAAAaaaaGGGGGgggghhh-hhh!!!!*" Why? Because, as he was speaking, the tiny partridge had deliberately, and with lightning speed, lunged at his eye, pecking it directly on the soft cornea with its tiny yet surprisingly sharp beak.

With that in mind, you'll probably agree that "at *AAAAaaaaGGGGGgggghhhhhh!!!!*" was a relatively sensible way for Dean Grumpf to finish the sentence.

Chapter 23

HENRY WALKED QUICKLY home through the cold, gray Harlem evening, his shoulders hunched against the drizzling rain.

After the disastrous meeting, he had offered to accompany Dean Grumpf and Provost Fringe to the school medical center. His offer was loudly declined by Dean Grumpf, who left clutching his eye and shouting very unsympathetic things about bird-kind.

Instead, Henry went to his office and tried to diligently read his students' essays. Flicking through several, he gave up, having reached the depressing conclusion that the C+ he'd given most of them was actually too generous.

Arriving home and entering his house,

Henry immediately noticed several new structures in his living room. These were the result of his children's trip to the home-improvement store with Mariana.

He had expected some small, unobtrusive, rudimentary hutches for the birds. Instead, he saw what could only be described as luxury bird hotels. His drinks cabinet had been pushed to the side and replaced by a large, two-tier wood-and-wire chicken coop with ramp and roosting bench. Where a tall floor lamp had been was a new birdhouse in the form of a colonial mansion with a long perch where the two doves were cooing happily...which is exactly what Henry would do, too, if he lived mortgage-free in a colonial mansion.

The calling birds' iron cage was in the hallway, hooked up to a watering system piped in from the guest bathroom. And on his shelves, where his books had been, were multiple containers of various forms of bird food. In the middle of this new arrangement, Will was on the sofa watching TV.

"How much did all this cost?!" Henry demanded.

"All the receipts are right there," replied Will, pointing to a crumpled mass of papers on the table.

Flicking through the first few, Henry's chin dropped and he exclaimed, "You only had to make shelters, not the Taj Mahal. How could it possibly cost this much?"

"It is what it is, Dad," said Will unhelpfully. "You want them to be comfortable, don't you?"

"Not more comfortable than *me*. My God, seventy-five dollars on *locusts*?"

"They're for the turtle doves," said Ella, who had been safely upstairs in her bird- and germ-free bedroom sanctuary when she heard her father come home.

"Locusts? What are they—dipped in truffles and rolled in caviar?!"

"This particular species of dove only eats Amazonian long-toed locusts, which are super hard to find," said Will.

"The Amazonian *short*-toed and *mid*-toed locusts are a dime a dozen, but the *long*-toed locust is very rare," explained Ella to her dad.

Henry, exasperated, looked at his children,

wondering how they knew so much about the price of locusts. And why. He dropped down into his favorite comfy chair and bounced immediately back up again with a strange yowl. He looked around to see a French hen in his seat.

"Get off!" he said, roughly brushing it onto the floor. "But why did you put them all in my living room? Put them in the kitchen."

"Where we prepare our *food*? Uh, I don't think so," Ella chastised.

"Then the dining room," suggested Henry.

"Right next to the kitchen where we prepare our food? No way."

"Dad." Will stopped him. "Don't even bother. I tried. This is the only place she'd allow them."

An annoyed Henry started to walk away. But Ella stopped him.

"How did your disciplinary review go?" Ella asked.

"Not great."

"Why not?" Will asked.

"Because of this little turd." He produced the partridge chick from his pocket.

"*That's* where he was. We were wondering," said Will, surprised by feeling a deep sense of relief.

"Turns out, he stowed away in my coat pocket. Then, midmeeting, decided to make an appearance and peck Dean Grumpf...*on the eyeball.*"

Both Will and Ella winced at the thought of that.

"Yes. Exactly. So, no, it didn't go well."

Henry walked over to the bookshelf, where he found the shoebox home that Ella had made for the partridge chick. Dropping him (or her) in, Henry leaned his face close to the bird's beak and angrily whispered, "That stunt of yours might have cost me my job."

Henry paused for a moment and savored the image of Dean Grumpf's expression as he hopped about clutching his eye and screaming. Then, making sure no one was watching, he placed an extra-large pinch of mealworms into the chick's bowl.

"Right," said Henry in a determined manner as he turned to face his children, "I'm going to end this once and for all with Ms. Truelove."

He was stopped, however, when Will said, "Hey, Dad, you know, if she *really* is giving us the gifts from 'The Twelve Days of Christmas,' then tomorrow is...five golden rings. Maybe wait a day?"

Chapter 24

HENRY DID WAIT. But not a day. Nor even an hour. He waited only long enough to pour and drink a large glass of brandy, which helped dissipate a lot of the pent-up anger he had been holding on to. With the dating website up on his computer screen, he typed,

> Dear Ms. Truelove. I don't know how much more specific I can be. But please… seriously… I beg of you… no more "gifts." Whatever you might have in mind for tomorrow—no matter how nice you might think it is—just please don't send it. If you do, I will be forced to take steps.

Henry pressed SEND and hoped for an end to this whole miserable misadventure.

On the Fifth Day

Chapter 25

ELLA LOOKED AT herself in the mirror over the old carved wooden mantelpiece in the living room and went down her checklist: Oven mitts? Check. Earmuffs? Check. Woolen hat? Check. Ski goggles? Check. Surgical mask? Check. Turtleneck pulled up over the chin? Check.

Ella was ready.

To climb the North Face of Everest? To orbit the earth in a space capsule? To inspect the remains of the Fukushima nuclear reactor? No, she was ready to clean the calling birds' cage.

Under Henry's mandate, Ella and Will were responsible for all chores related to Ms. Truelove's gifts. They had divided up the tasks by flipping a coin, and Ella got the calling birds and the partridge while Will got the French hens and turtle doves.

"You look ridiculous," said Will, staring at Ella's improvised protective outfit.

"Not as ridiculous as you'll look when you catch some kind of flesh-eating bacteria from those hens and half your face is missing as they gnaw through your soft tissue, leaving a gaping bloody hole," Ella shot back.

"Where do you *get* this stuff?" Will stared.

"Internet." Ella shrugged.

The new chores added precious minutes to Will and Ella's daily preschool routine when they'd much rather be sleeping. Will completed his tasks while muttering angrily about stupid birds. Ella tried to complete her tasks while holding her breath the entire time, in an effort to avoid inhaling any foreign bird microbes that could wreak havoc with her insides. Once done, she threw her clothes into the battered old washing machine on a hot-hot cycle and ran straight into the shower to scrub off any particularly determined germs that might have inveigled their way through her protective layers.

She was just finishing dressing and running a bleach wipe across her bedroom furniture handles and surfaces when she heard the doorbell ring. By now, all three Sullivans had an involuntary, Pavlovian response to the doorbell that involved a shiver and goose bumps.

"Delivery!" a voice shouted from outside.

"I got this," Henry told his children as he approached the front door, clutching a baseball bat in his hands.

When Henry opened the door, however, the deliveryman and his truck were, once again, nowhere to be seen.

How could he be gone? He had rung the doorbell barely five seconds prior. Did the guy have wings? Was his delivery truck a particularly quiet helicopter or something?

Henry looked left and right. And left again. Nothing. Then he looked down, where he found the delivery itself. It was unlike the others that had arrived over the previous four days. This was a glossy, stiff, well-designed shopping bag in a rich deep purple with a generous swathe of silky white ribbon tied around the handles in a flamboyant bow.

"Open it, open it," urged Will, once Henry had brought it into the living room. "I think I know what it is," he sang excitedly.

"Let me," said Ella, taking the bow between her thumb and forefinger. It glided open with the gentlest of tugs.

Inside the bag was a long, thin gift, swathed in luxurious purple paper. Ella carefully tore it open along the taped seams to reveal a velvet box, also rich purple in color.

The Sullivans looked at each other.

Will and Ella were almost giddy with excitement. Henry took a deep breath and flipped the hinged top open, half expecting something horrifically inconvenient to come flying out.

But nothing did.

Inside the box, slotted into the silken base, were...

"Five golden rings! Just like the song. I knew it," shouted Will triumphantly. "You think they're real?"

Henry took a ring out of its slot and peered at the inside of it, where 18K was clearly stamped.

"They're real," confirmed Henry.

"Now, *that's* more like it," Will exclaimed. "It might have taken her a while to get around to the good gifts. But on the fifth day, Ms. Truelove gave us five golden rings!"

"She also gave us four calling birds."

"Three French hens."

"Two turtle doves."

"And a partridge."

"In a pear tree." Ella smiled.

"Let's not get ahead of ourselves. We don't actually know for sure that these rings are from her," cautioned Henry.

"Who else has sent us a gift in the last five years?" Will said flatly. "And it's the next gift from the song."

"I'm just saying, there's not a card or anything," explained Henry.

"It's from her, all right," Ella said, pointing at the interior lid of the box.

Will read the words printed in flowery gold letters. "*Groot Liefde & Co. Amsterdam. Purveyors of fine jewels to the rich, famous and dangerously overextended.* So?"

"In Dutch, *groot* means 'great' or 'true.'

Liefde means 'love.'" Ella pointed to the screen on her laptop. "The rings are from True Love & Co."

Henry shook his head angrily. "I asked her not to send us anything more."

"You're angry at her for sending us five golden rings?" asked Will incredulously.

"I'm angry at her for doing what I told her not to. We don't want her gifts. We don't want her interference in our lives. She's a crazy lady," Henry said. "And what comes next?"

"Uh, six geese, I believe," said Ella.

"Exactly. You want geese? I don't want geese."

"She can't send us geese. Where is she going to get geese from?"

"I don't know. Canada?" said Henry, standing up and looking determined.

"What are you going to do?" Ella asked.

"Don't worry about it," Henry replied, grabbing his coat and heading out the door, pausing only long enough to check for a partridge in his pockets.

Chapter 26

"Ya say dese were 'gifts'?" the pawnbroker asked, making air quotes with his fingers.

A lot of things had changed in Harlem over the past twenty years. But there was still a proliferation of pawnbrokers willing to take advantage of any reversal of fortune. They all had an abundance of security cameras and buzzer systems that only allowed a customer into the store after inspection. This one had a number of musical instruments in the window as well as slightly outdated recording equipment. But inside there were glass cabinets full of jewelry and watches.

"They *were* gifts," answered Henry. "You don't have to make air quotes."

From the moment he opened the box,

Henry had decided to sell the rings. Their sale would cover all his Truelove-related expenses and still leave him with a little left over to help with some small repairs around the house that he had been meaning to get to.

"Ya got a receipt?" the man asked suspiciously, removing a jeweler's loupe from his eye.

"No, I don't have a receipt. As I said, they were a gift," said Henry somewhat impatiently.

"So ya said. Who gave 'em to ya?"

"A friend."

"That's a pretty good friend that gives ya five gold rings from a fancy European jeweler."

"I guess so."

"Then why ya sellin' 'em?"

"Why does anyone sell anything? I'd rather have the money than the rings. Now, how much will you give me for them?"

"Zero," said the man, pushing the box back across the counter while scratching his belly.

"Is this a negotiating tactic? You say zero. I say a million dollars. Then we haggle down to a reasonable price?"

"Nope. I'm not interested."

"Yeah, okay, I get it," said Henry knowingly. "Let's haggle. What's your starting offer?"

"Nuttin'."

"You know there are a lot of pawnbrokers out there who would jump at the chance to buy quality jewelry like this."

"Why don't you go to one o' dem?"

"Because… because it's cold and wet outside and I'd rather just sell them to you now," Henry lied. The truth was, he'd been to six other pawnbrokers already. And had received the same suspicious response from each. It was like another cruel trick from Ms. Truelove.

"Just give me a thousand dollars," suggested Henry. "That's a bargain."

"Nah."

"Nine hundred."

"They're stolen, ain't they?"

"Eight hundred."

"They're getting hotter, buddy."

And so was Henry.

"Seven hundred dollars!" Henry shouted. "That's practically free! Each individual ring must be worth at least seven hundred and I'm offering you all five for that!"

"Calm down, pal."

"Calm down? How can I calm down? I'm begging some idiot to give me six hundred dollars for what could be thousands of dollars' worth of fine jewelry. It's infuriating. Absurd! Perverse! Tell me, sir, with that kind of business sense, how do you manage to keep this place open?" asked Henry while gesturing to the shop interior with a sweeping outstretched arm.

In doing so, however, Henry accidentally knocked over a wooden coat stand, which—seemingly in slow motion—dropped into a display case of gold watches, smashing the glass and setting off an earsplitting alarm. Henry looked down in horror at the million shattered, glinting shards. When he looked up again at the pawnbroker, he found himself staring at the glinting steel barrel of a Magnum .45 gun. Henry raised his hands slowly and smiled weakly.

Chapter 27

DESPITE INSISTING THAT literally everyone on the planet had one, Will could not convince his dad to buy him a mobile phone. So Will found himself still dependent on the house landline for his social life, which, although currently fairly dire, he was hoping would improve soon. He was therefore gratified to hear Cuz and Noodle's voices when he answered the phone that afternoon.

"Hey, guys! How are you guys? What are you up to? What's up? I'm glad you called. I was just hanging out," Will babbled, the words tumbling clumsily out of his mouth.

"Hey, Will. We need you to do something for us."

"Yeah, sure. Whatever," Will said, trying to regain an air of coolness.

"Meet us in the alley behind the school at 3 p.m. tomorrow."

"At 3 p.m. I have social studies, so I'll be—"

"Are you our friend or not, Will?" Noodle interrupted. "Because if you're our friend, you'll meet us there."

"Yeah, I'm your friend, sure. Of course. It's just—"

"Good," Cuz cut him off. "I knew you wouldn't let us down. See you there."

With that, Cuz and Noodle hung up.

Will wondered what they needed him for. More shoplifting? To be a lookout? To drive a getaway car? Or maybe they just needed help with their homework. Although he was a grade behind them, he was pretty sure they all acknowledged that he was smarter than them. Will didn't have long to think about it, though, because at that moment, the doorbell rang.

Will and Ella came out of their bedrooms at the same time, meeting on the landing.

"You think it's another delivery?" Ella asked with dread in her voice.

"I hope so. More gold, please," he responded.

They opened the door to see that it was indeed a delivery. Sort of. But not the kind they had imagined. The deliverymen were police. And their delivery was Henry.

Instead of returning with a pile of cash as he had intended, Henry had returned with yet *another* hefty fine. This time for public nuisance. It could have been so much worse. But luckily the pawnbroker was sympathetic to mental health issues and took pity on Henry, whom he assumed was wrestling with internal demons.

Henry, however, was wrestling with just one demon: Ms. Truelove.

Chapter 28

SEEING THEIR FATHER brought home by the police was a bit of a wake-up call for Will and Ella. He had looked so defeated, and they couldn't help feeling somewhat responsible. Mainly because they were *entirely* responsible. After all, they *had* invited Ms. Truelove into their lives.

So, that night, while Henry was upstairs consoling himself one glass at a time, downstairs Will and Ella logged back on to the dating website and found the twenty-four-hour help line number.

They took a moment to giggle over what sort of dating emergencies necessitated a *twenty-four-hour* help line: *Help! She has spinach stuck in her teeth. Should I tell her or not?!... Help!*

He just revealed he has fifteen cats and each is named after a famous murderer!...Help! She arrived to our first date in a wedding dress. Is that a red flag?

Having exhausted their list of comedy dating emergencies, Will picked up the phone and dialed. After he was on hold listening to bad music for what seemed like an eternity, a female voice finally answered.

"Hello. Splice dot com dating site. How can we help?"

"We're looking for a user who calls herself Ms. Truelove. Can you give us her real name, phone number, and address, please?" Will asked.

"No," replied the voice. "I certainly cannot."

"I thought this was a help line. That's not very helpful," Will shot back.

"I'm sorry, but we have to protect the identity of our members. May I ask why you want her information?"

"Because she's a crazy lady."

"Oh. Right. I see. Would you like to lodge a complaint against her? I can certainly officially censure her for you. And if it continues, we would suspend her account entirely."

Ella leaned into the receiver. "You really won't just give us her information so we can take care of this directly?"

"No."

"Then, okay, let's do the censure and suspension thing. That'll at least send a message."

The representative asked for the user's profile name again.

"Ms. Truelove," said Will.

They waited while they heard rapid typing on the other end of the line. Finally, the voice spoke again.

"I don't see a Ms. Truelove. Are you sure it's Ms. and not Miss or Mrs. or Madam or Madame or Mistress Truelove?"

Will confirmed that it was indeed Ms. Truelove and even spelled *Truelove*.

The representative kept typing rapidly. After an exhaustive search and discussion about the various options and spellings, she sighed deeply and said, "I'm afraid there is no profile for a Ms. Truelove. And there never has been. I've looked back through all our records."

"But there must be," insisted Ella. "She sent us messages on your site. We wrote back."

The representative paused, then asked, "I don't mean to jump to conclusions, but are you two a couple of kids?"

"Yes," admitted Ella, "we are. But we made the profile for our father, who is useless at dating."

"Which is why he *asked us* to help," Will added, hoping to lend their situation some legitimacy.

The representative seemed satisfied and asked what profile name they used for their father.

"HandsomeFunnyCharmingSmartAvailableNow5000," replied Ella.

"The *five thousand* was my idea," Will added. "Makes him sound cooler, doesn't it?"

"Much cooler," the representative dead-panned as she typed.

"See," Will said to Ella.

"Ah. Here we are. I think I've found it," the representative said. "The, uh ... tango-dancing race-car driver?"

"That's the one. Why? You interested?"

"No. And you said you messaged back and forth with Ms. Truelove via the Splice dot com internal messaging system?"

"Uh-huh."

The representative's tone took a sharp, angry turn. "Are you guys just messing with me? I have other lonely people who need real help, you know."

Will and Ella insisted that they were being genuine.

"But you never activated your account. You never paid for it. So you could not have received or sent any form of communication with other users."

"That's what we thought, too," said Ella, "but her messages came through. And we wrote back. Several times…"

"I'd like to help and I wish you guys well with your dad. But there's clearly been some kind of mistake. It must have been a different dating site. Either way, there is no Ms. Truelove here, and even if there was, you could not have messaged with her."

With that, the representative hung up. Instead of clearing up issues and leading them to Ms. Truelove's true identity, the call had only left Will and Ella more freaked out than ever.

On the Sixth Day

Chapter 29

TROUBLED BY THE many unanswered questions that arose from their conversation with the help-line lady, Ella had not slept well. Subsequently, she spent the morning in something of a haze. Luckily, if you're generally quiet, nobody notices when you're extra quiet, so people left her largely to herself, which was how Ella liked it anyway.

By lunchtime, Ella was back in the school theater painting her backgrounds. The creative outlet gave Ella her first feeling of peace since she had hung up the phone the previous night. She allowed herself to get lost in the painting and in the singing happening on-stage. She absently watched Sally Kensington in the middle of another solo performance.

Say what you like about Sally, she knew how to knock a show tune out of the park. Ella was roused from her dreamlike state by her friend Suzanne, who had been painting alongside her.

"Hey," whispered Suzanne. "Is something up? You seem distracted."

"Me?" Ella whispered back. "No. Why do you ask?"

"You've painted six legs on that horse," Suzanne responded, pointing to the horse and a half. "What's going on?"

Ella debated internally whether to open up to Suzanne. On the one hand, she did not want to sound insane. On the other, Suzanne was the kind of logical, thoughtful person who might be able to offer up a rational explanation. Nothing about Ms. Truelove was either explicable or rational as far as Ella could deduce. Surely a sensible outsider like Suzanne—without bias or preconceptions—could shed some light on the whole situation.

So Ella put down her paintbrush, took a moment to compose her thoughts, and began to tell the tale in a barely audible low whisper.

"Okay...so...my brother and I built a dating profile for our dad in order to find him a wife so he would be happy again and, to be honest, in the hope that we'd start getting Christmas presents again. Well, a woman on the dating website messaged us. But our dad caught us red-handed and was not happy about it. So he wrote to her to tell her that he wasn't interested. And the next morning BAWK BAWK SQUAWK BA-CAW BAWK!!!"

Eyes wide, Ella slammed her hand over her mouth. *What in God's name,* she wondered, *just happened?* Ella had spontaneously and involuntarily begun squawking like a chicken. Suzanne wondered, too. As did some of the stagehands working closest to them. Sally Kensington—ever the professional—darted an angry look toward the wings but managed not to skip a beat of her song.

"What was *that?*" Suzanne whispered. "Are you okay?"

Ella nodded her head and slowly took her

hands away from her mouth. No noises came out. She waited another moment to see if it would happen again. It didn't. So, sufficiently reassured, she decided to ignore the outburst and resume her story.

"Sorry about that. Strange. Anyway, to cut a long story short, over the past five days, the woman has sent us BAWK BAWK SQUAWK BA-BAWK SQUAWK!!!"

Again! Even louder! And longer. And with even less control.

What was going on?! One bird-noise outburst could have been some kind of involuntary bodily mishap, like chicken hiccups or avian sneeze or something. But twice? And *exactly* when she was going to talk about the gifts!

This was more than a coincidence or a spasm. This was somehow the work of Ms. Truelove. Ella didn't know how or why. But this was another piece of Truelove-esque magic. Like the deliverymen who disappeared far too quickly. Or the birds that reappeared in their living room after being dropped off in the forest. Or the messages from someone who doesn't exist on a website they hadn't paid for. The impossible was becoming not only possible but positively *common* in the Sullivan family's lives.

Ella had tried to tell Suzanne the story in order to gain some perspective, logic, and lucidity. But she had only managed to instill more doubt and confusion in her own mind.

Ella shuddered at the control Ms. Truelove exerted over them. And then shuddered a second time at the thought of what might come next. Had Ella *actually* known what was to come over the next several days, she would have shuddered a third, fourth, and fifth time.

"How...*dare* you disturb an artist midperformance," Sally breathed out ominously. Ella looked up to find Sally standing, hands on hips, looking down on her. "Do you think you're being funny or something?"

Suzanne had already taken refuge behind the set. Ms. Conti, on the other hand, rolled her eyes and dropped into a chair to watch the offstage performance. Ella shook her head silently but vigorously.

"Who are you? What are you doing here?" Sally hissed.

"I'm Ella," Ella squeaked, her voice softly quavering. "I'm painting the sets." She pointed weakly to her work.

Looking at the well-crafted work Ella had designed and painstakingly painted, Sally pursed her lips off to one side as if formulating an opinion.

"They all have to go," she finally decreed.

"Huh?" Ella grunted.

"Yeah. All new sets. These are no good."

"What...what do you mean, 'no good'?"

"I mean," Sally enunciated. "They. Are. Not. Good."

"Why?"

"All the sets need to be...blue," declared Sally Kensington.

"Blue? But the musical is... *White Christmas.*"

"Listen, I don't know who you think you are, but people are paying good money to come and see *me* sing. And when I was on *America's Got Talent,* the makeup lady told me to surround myself with blue because blue really makes my eyes pop." Then Sally asked suspiciously, "Do you *not* want my eyes to pop?"

"No," Ella whispered, "of course I want your eyes to pop."

"Then we need new sets. All blue. That's the only color you'll use. It'll be modern. It'll be stark. It'll be groundbreaking. And, most importantly, it'll make my eyes pop! Now, do it!"

With that, Sally returned to the stage and resumed her duet with Gus Gustavson as if she hadn't just told someone to redesign and repaint dozens of entirely new sets for a five-act musical just six days before the opening night.

"Dude," Suzanne whispered, coming out from behind a panel. "That was intense."

"Yeah," replied Ella. "I'll come back tomorrow with new designs, but we'll have to work quickly."

"That's not what I meant. I was talking about the...squawking?"

"It was nothing. I just...had something stuck in my throat and was trying to get it out," Ella covered.

"Ella…" Suzanne started.

"Seriously. That was it."

"Okay," said Suzanne, unconvinced. "Then go on. Tell me what the woman from the website did."

"Sure. Fine. She…wasn't interested in my dad and she was the only lead we had so that's it." Ella had to end this conversation. "I gotta go. See you tomorrow," she said as she gathered her coat and gloves and stumbled toward the exit.

Chapter 30

WILL WAS UNUSUALLY quiet that day, too. Firstly, like Ella, he was still freaked out about their call with the online dating company. And, secondly, he had no idea how he was going to get out of Mr. Fitzatelli's class to meet his friends. They were relying on him and he couldn't let them down. But there was no way to get out of class without being caught.

"Sullivan!" Mr. Fitzatelli shouted.

"Julius Caesar!" Will shouted instinctively, snapping out of his own world of distant thoughts and worries. Then added, just in case, "The Battle of Marathon! . . . Cleopatra . . . the Minotaur?"

The class laughed. Mr. Fitzatelli, the football coach and social studies teacher, told them to be quiet. He approached Will, who braced himself for some kind of punishment. Instead, however, Mr. Fitzatelli took Will to one side and asked if he wasn't feeling well.

"I mean, you're unusually quiet today. You sick? Or is there something going on at home?" asked Mr. Fitzatelli, who could be surprisingly emotionally perceptive for an ex-jock.

Taking advantage of Mr. Fitzatelli's kindness, Will seized the opportunity and croaked sickly, "Yes. I feel sick. Can I go see the school nurse?"

Eager for any excuse to get the disruptive Will out of his classroom, Mr. Fitzatelli gladly permitted him to go.

Behind the school in a secluded city alleyway, among the garbage cans and trash, were Cuz, Noodle, Bean, and Fash. When they caught sight of the approaching Will, they greeted him with smacks on the back, congratulating him for skipping stupid social studies to do something cool and fun. Will smiled shyly, enjoying the attention.

"So, what are we doing?" Will asked.

"See that window up there?" Fash said, pointing to a small window up one story.

When Will confirmed that he did, Bean explained that behind the window was Mr. Fitzatelli's office. And in his office were all the exam papers for grades nine and ten. They also happened to know that the lock was broken on that particular window. So, if someone small and light could shimmy up the drainpipe to it, that person would be able to gain access to the room and make copies of the exams.

"Why not go in through the door?" Will suggested.

"Because the door is locked. We're not stupid," huffed Cuz.

"Oh," said Will, looking up. "The window is pretty small. I guess that rules out Noodle," he joked.

"Yeah, totally. And Bean and I are too heavy for the drainpipe," said Fash.

"So it's me or Cuz?" Will nodded.

"It would be, but Cuz has a real problem with heights," said Bean.

"It's true. I do. I get all dizzy and stuff,"

confirmed Cuz, adding, "I barfed during the school trip to the Empire State Building."

"So," said Will, putting two and two together, "you want *me* to do it?"

"It'll be so cool, dude, climbing up there, breaking in, getting the goods," said Noodle.

The others joined in talking about how they wished they could do it and how lucky Will was that he was the only one with the necessary size, skills, and all-out badassery to pull off the heist. Before he even knew what was happening, Will found himself being lifted onto the dumpster so he could grab hold of the drainpipe that led vertically up the flat brick wall toward the window.

"He keeps the exams in his desk," said Fash, pushing Will up the drainpipe.

"He doesn't lock the desk because he locks the office door and that's the only way in," added Bean.

"Or so he thinks!" Cuz cheered. "But we're smarter than him. Now, go on. Hurry."

Will looked up at the path he'd have to take. The drainpipe rattled ominously when he shook it. Several of the bolts holding it into the wall were worryingly rusty and loose. This would have been an excellent time to say no, but seemingly lifted by a tail-wind of his friends' expectation, Will merely reached up high to heave himself up the drainpipe.

"W-w-what are you doing, Will?" said a new voice.

They all looked around to see Benny's head sticking out of another window.

"Go away, Benny. This is none of your business," hissed Will.

"Are you c-climbing up the drainpipe?"

"Yeah, so what?" Cuz said. "Will isn't afraid. He's not a little stuttering baby like you."

"Go back inside, Benny," instructed Will.

"If you f-fall, you could r-really hurt yourself."

"He's not gonna fall," said Noodle. "Are you, Will?"

"No. I'm not. Now go *away*, Benny," Will insisted.

"But, W-Will..."

"Ugh, Benny, leave me alone. This is why we're not friends anymore. 'Cause you didn't grow up and grow a pair. I have new friends and you're just jealous. Now GO AWAY."

"And don't tell anyone!" Fash shouted after him. "Or we'll beat your ass."

"D-don't worry, I w-won't," said Benny, who withdrew his head from the window, looking at Will imploringly the whole way.

Benny disappeared back inside and all sense of reason went with him. A riled-up Will was now free to embark on the perilous trek up the wall. He managed to pull himself up the drainpipe slowly, hand over hand, while using the iron brackets as footholds. The pipe rattled and creaked. But Will persisted, urged on by the hoots and cheers of his friends standing safely on solid ground below. By some miracle, he eventually arrived at the edge of the window. He looked down briefly, which was a mistake. The ground seemed very far away and, somehow, especially *hard*. Taking a deep breath and shifting his weight, Will reached out for the window. As he did, his foot slipped off a bracket and he started to fall. His heart leaped up into his throat. Every molecule in his body tensed up. Acting purely on adrenaline and instinct, Will somehow clung on and managed to hook an elbow securely over the concrete sill just in time. He could hear the group below let out a sigh of relief.

"Dude! Get in. Don't just hang there!" one of them shouted.

Panting, Will pulled himself up and pushed open the window before crawling inside and collapsing on the carpet, sweating, his heart pounding. He could hear the four guys down below whispering anxiously so he poked his head out of the window and gave them a weak thumbs-up.

Will then started searching the drawers in Mr. Fitzatelli's desk and very quickly found the exam papers. Just as quickly, he photocopied them, shoved the copies inside his jacket pocket, and replaced the originals exactly as he'd found them. He'd done it. He was surely a full member of the gang now.

Will opened the window again. "Got 'em!"

The members of the band outside fist-bumped and shoved each other excitedly. Cuz told Will to get out of there and to make sure he locked the door again after him when he left. They'd be waiting in the alley. But when Will twisted the door handle to leave, he discovered it was locked with a key and that key would be needed to unlock it. He rattled the handle, pulling and twisting with all his might. But it wouldn't budge. He was locked inside. Worse, he could hear approaching voices on the other side of the door. He was stuck in the office with no place to hide. As the voices got closer, he could clearly make out Mr. Fitzatelli's distinctive Brooklyn rumble. Will ran back to the window.

"I can't get out!" Will whisper-shouted. "You need a key to unlock the door! And Mr. Fitzatelli is coming!"

"Climb down the pipe," instructed a worried-looking Bean.

"It's too far away. I can't reach it," Will said. Then, thinking quickly, Will pointed to the dumpster. "If you guys climb up on there, I can probably hang from the windowsill and drop if you guys will catch me. It won't be that far. Will you guys catch me?"

"Throw down the exams," replied Noodle.

"Climb up, guys," said Will with one leg out of the window.

"How close is Fitzatelli?" Cuz asked.

"He's at the door!! Hurry! Climb up," Will urged them, his heart racing again.

But the guys didn't climb up. And they didn't catch him. And they didn't suggest an alternate escape for Will. They just ran.

"Guys! *Guys!!*...GUYS!!!!"

But Will was shouting at the heels of their stolen sneakers as they hightailed it out of there and far away.

Chapter 31

THE FOUR MINUTES from the school's front door to Henry's car was more of a death march than a walk. Will and Ella had never seen their father look so angry. And they'd seen him angry a *lot*. Like the time Ella swatted a fly on his bare foot…with a hammer. Or the time Henry dropped his passport down a sewage drain outside the airport. Or the time Will drew a rocket ship on page seventeen of the leather-bound, first-edition Charles Dickens book that Henry had saved up all year to buy for their mother. Or the time his barber sneezed while cutting his hair, giving Henry a reverse Mohawk. Or the time the family went to a petting zoo and a llama spat in his face at the exact moment he was yawning. Or the time…you get the picture. Henry was angry a lot.

But those times were nothing like this time. Because those times, he shouted and swore, jumped and railed. But this time, he opted for a silence so chilling that a penguin might have asked for earmuffs and a cashmere scarf.

Will and Ella weren't sure which was more firmly clenched, Henry's jaw or his fists.

Either way, Henry did not need words to make the magnitude of his displeasure perfectly clear. It was somehow in his every movement and gesture. The simple act of opening the car door seemed to say, "I'm disappointed in you." The way he turned on the engine somehow screamed, "How could you be so stupid?" And crisply clicking his seat belt was the equivalent of pointing at Will and shouting, "You are grounded forever."

While Will sat in the front passenger seat staring down at his shoes, Ella was sitting quietly in the back seat. She had planned to tell Will and her dad about the disturbing squawking episode, but this was clearly not the time. They were about halfway home, however, when she suddenly got the uncomfortable feeling of someone watching her. So, while the three of them drove along in frosty silence, Ella slowly swiveled her head around and saw that someone was indeed watching her. Actually, not some*one*. Rather, some*thing*.

A goose. A long-necked, black-beaked, brown-feathered, beady-eyed goose.

It had poked its head up over the back seat from the trunk area of the SUV and was looking at her in what could only be described as a pugnacious manner.

"Uhhh…dad?" Ella said, attempting to break the ice with a gentle tap.

"Ella. I'm too angry to talk," Henry, eyes fixed on the road ahead, stopped her. "I'm genuinely afraid of what I'll say if I start."

"I know, but, Dad…" Ella said, not taking her eyes off the goose, who had been joined by five more curious compadres. For a total of six geese. Just like the song promised.

"Not now, Ella!" Henry barked sharply, causing everyone in the car to jump. And by "everyone," I mean *everyone,* including the geese, who, in their shock, began honking at the top of their lungs. The shock of the honks, in turn, caused Henry to jump and inadvertently drive up onto the curb and into a mailbox, deeply scratching the entire length of his SUV with a wince-inducing metallic scraping sound.

Henry slammed on the brakes, and now Will and Ella were witness to the kind of angry outburst they were more used to from Henry. The steering wheel bore the brunt of his fury as he railed against geese, noise, cars, and the United States Postal Service, but mostly against Ms. Truelove.

Meanwhile, Ella looked back past the geese and noticed a tall tower of empty egg cartons marked "TRUELOVE FREE RANGE GOOSE EGGS." Ms. Truelove seemed to be a stickler for details. She didn't just send geese. She sent geese who would be *a-laying*.

On the Seventh Day

Chapter 32

HENRY STRODE PURPOSEFULLY down Frederick Douglass Boulevard past the patchwork of old and new shop fronts. It was another cold gray day. Snow had again been promised by the weather people, but they were again wrong. There was just the piercing wind that swirled down New York's wide boulevards lined with tall buildings, causing chins to sink into necks and shoulders to reach up toward ears.

The previous night, the Sullivans had managed to herd the snapping geese from the garage into the house and up to the upstairs bathroom. Will dashed in quickly to run a few inches of water in the bathtub and leave a heap of seeds on the floor in the corner. Although fiercely nipped and honked at, he managed to escape intact but sported a number of sore, red beak-shaped welts on his skin under his clothes. But it was a small price to pay, he thought, for redirecting his father's attentions.

If ever you are in trouble with your parents—*real* trouble—you should try surprising them with a half dozen waterfowl with bad attitudes and sharp beaks. You will find that it quickly takes the focus off of your indiscretions. Henry had by no means forgotten about Will's stupid stunt. And Henry would not, for a long time, forget having to beg the headmaster to downgrade Will's expulsion to suspension for the rest of the semester. But, for the moment, Henry had wild geese on his mind. And, of course, Ms. Truelove.

Once the geese had been safely corralled into the bathroom, Will and Ella came clean to their father about their troubling conversation with the dating website. Seeing how worried they were by it, he sighed and, after a moment's thought, suggested that Ms. Truelove must have somehow hacked their internet feed or something, bypassing the dating website's server and plugging straight into theirs. Although only a guess, it offered his children some welcome relief as it was the first rational explanation they'd heard.

Although Henry had maintained a calm facade, internally he was vexed. If he was right about the hacking, it was a major escalation in the bizarre menace of Ms. Truelove. He kept his concerns to himself because he did not want to worry his children any further. And, of course, because the Sullivan family—led by his own poor example—simply didn't share emotions or feelings.

Henry was sure of one thing, though. This was the last of her gifts. According to the song, swans come next. And no matter how hard it is to come by French hens or geese, swans are surely nearly impossible to buy and have de-livered. All the same, Henry had warned Ms. Truelove in his last message that if she sent any more gifts, he would be forced to take action. And that action had him striding down Freder-ick Douglass Boulevard, turning sharply onto 135th Street and up the steps to the New York City Police Department's 32nd Precinct.

He had hoped to keep the situation between themselves. He had hoped that he could reason with Ms. Truelove. But that had proved itself to be impossible. And if he had to go to the law, it was entirely Ms. Truelove's own doing. He had tried being nice. Or at least *his version* of being nice, which wasn't actually particularly nice. But she had ignored him. And now she had to face the consequences of her own actions. Henry didn't like to involve the police, but he could see no alternative. If this led to her indictment and incarceration, then so be it.

Maybe, Henry reasoned, this was for the best. Maybe Ms. Truelove needed this wake-up call. Or needed help. Psychiatric help. To stop her harming herself or others. And, if nothing else, the police would have the resources to finally identify the person who had turned the Sullivans' world upside down.

As much as Henry wanted to put the whole episode behind himself and go back to how things were, he had to admit that he had a gnawing curiosity about who was behind all of it. And how on God's green earth she had managed to do everything. Now, with the assistance of the limitless resources of the police, he would finally find out.

With this in mind, Henry strode inside the police station, presented himself in a deter-mined manner to the desk sergeant, and, in a strong voice, said...

"Excuse me, but *ngingathanda ukubika ubugebengu.*"

Henry clenched his mouth shut as his eyes popped wide-open. *What the hell did I just say?* he thought. He had meant to say, "I would like to report a crime." But that is not what came out.

"Eeerrrrrr, what's that?" the overweight ser-geant asked, looking up from his crime novel.

Henry shook his head, cleared his throat, and tried again, "Excuse me. What I meant to say was...*ngingathanda ukubika ubugebengu.*"

Like Ella had done the day before, Henry, too, clapped his hand over his mouth. Henry, of course, had no idea that this is exactly what happened when Ella tried to tell Suzanne about Ms. Truelove because, as mentioned previously, the Sullivans—to their detriment—did not share emotions and feelings.

The only difference was that, instead of squawking, Henry was somehow speaking an obscure, distantly foreign language. Possibly a sub-Saharan African dialect, Henry thought, trying to remember what he could of an African Civilization class he took while studying for his doctorate. The exact location of the language's origin, however, was considerably less of a concern than... *THAT HE WAS SPEAKING A LANGUAGE HE DIDN'T KNOW OR UNDERSTAND WHILE TRYING TO SAY SOMETHING IN ENGLISH.*

Henry had experienced a number of strange things over the past few days, but the loss of his ability to speak his native tongue was, by far, the most disturbing yet.

"You been drinking, pal?" the sergeant asked, staring at Henry.

"No!" Henry insisted before admitting, "Well, yes, a drop in my coffee, but it's a cold day and I walked here, so..." Henry stopped, pleased to notice that he was speaking English again. Maybe the weirdness was over. With a smile and a relieved sigh, he began again, "So as I was saying... *owesifazane ku-intanethi.*"

He shut his mouth firmly again.

"Hey, Persky," the desk sergeant whispered to a passing rookie, "we got a psych case here. Call the on-duty shrink. I'll try to keep him calm."

Persky took one look at Henry and pulled the desk sergeant aside. "I think that's the guy I picked up for criminal damage at a pawn shop yesterday."

"Yeah?! Clearly a whack job. Let's, uh, 'invite' him in," the sergeant whispered, standing up and reaching for his handcuffs.

But Henry also recognized the rookie cop and didn't like the way they were whispering. So, by the time they looked back up for him, Henry was already gone, power walking back up Frederick Douglass Boulevard toward the pint bottle of Old Grand-Dad bourbon in the lower left desk drawer in his Hamilton Hall office.

Chapter 33

Speed walking with laser focus across the Columbia University campus, intent on reaching his office without delay, Henry was annoyed to hear a distinct "Henry! Henry!" He didn't need to look to know it was his friend, Dr. Hastings Fringe. Doing his best to pretend he didn't hear, Henry continued on his direct line toward the steps of Hamilton Hall. But Dr. Fringe was not one to be deterred. Henry felt a meaty hand on his shoulder.

"Henry, I've been calling out your name," said Dr. Fringe.

"Have you? Really? Sorry, Hastie. Didn't hear. Must be the wind," rambled a rattled Henry. "Well, nice to see you. Better be moving on."

Henry tried walking away from his friend only to be pulled back again.

"Henry, I really think we need to discuss your situation."

"My *situation*?"

"Yes. The 'situation' in which you might be fired. Or had you forgotten that Dean Grumpf is baying for your blood?" Dr. Fringe sighed. "What is going on, Henry? You've been acting very strangely. Be honest with me," he implored, looking at Henry with his large, kind brown eyes.

But, as much as he wanted to, Henry couldn't be honest. He couldn't risk trying to tell Dr. Fringe what had been going on in his life and in his house. Firstly, it sounded insane. And secondly, what if he started speaking in that sub-Saharan—possibly Sutu or Zulu, now that he thought about it—dialect again?

Henry swallowed and put his hand on Dr. Fringe's powerful arm. But before he could say anything, Henry made eye contact with something very disconcerting in the distance.

A swan.

There was a white swan staring at him

from across the South Lawn, a large, grassy expanse between the university's administrative buildings. A chill ran up the length of Henry's back like the signal from some kind of primordial early-warning system. With the Christmas carol—specifically the bit about seven swans a-swimming—ringing in his ears, Henry turned a sharp 180 degrees and began to walk in the opposite direction. Away from the swan.

"I gotta go," said Henry.

"I'll walk with you."

Striding alongside Henry, Fringe rambled on about the medical prognosis for Dean Grumpf's scratched cornea until he noticed Henry had stopped again with a slightly haunted look on his face. The reason for that look was that Henry had spotted a *second* swan. There was no mistaking it. The swan was definitely staring at him as if to say, "Found you." Henry did another rapid turn, heading up past the Columbia University Visitors Center. Fringe kept right on alongside him, airily recounting the tale of Dean Grumpf's examination by the eye specialist.

Henry didn't hear a word of it, though. He was on the lookout for swans. Thankfully, he didn't see any more and was pretty sure he'd given them the slip. After all, swans are not known for their tracking and hunting abilities. But just when he thought he was in the clear, he darted a look over his shoulder only to spot *four* of the creatures waddling roughly ten feet behind himself and Fringe. Henry stifled a cry and turned again, this time up the steps, past the columns, and into St. Paul's Chapel, Dr. Fringe alongside him the whole time.

"Why are we in here?" Fringe whispered, looking respectfully around.

"I like to have a quick…prayer session sometimes. For focus and guidance in being a better teacher," babbled Henry.

"Good. Must let Grumpf know. He's quite the religious—"

"Yaaah!" Henry exclaimed involuntarily, his voice echoing in the silence of the high ceiling. There were now *six* swans waddling down the transept toward them.

"What is it?" Fringe asked, looking squarely

at Henry and, thankfully, not toward the swans.

"I already prayed today. What am I thinking? Silly me," Henry said, shoving Fringe quite roughly back outside into the street and slamming the chapel's huge double doors after them. "Well, Hastie, it's been great to catch up. But I gotta go. So busy. I'll call you later. I do want to continue discussing whatever it was you were just talking about, which is extremely important to me," blathered Henry, overenthusiastically pumping Hastie's hand like he was sawing through a thick log. Dr. Fringe was left slightly confused as he watched Henry zigzag across campus, making several sharp turns, ducking behind trees, and periodically pirouetting to check behind himself until he finally disappeared down Amsterdam Avenue.

Henry continued his erratic path, which included hiding in shop entrances, pressing himself against the sides of buildings, and doubling back on himself several times. This might have attracted the stares of a lot of people, but Henry didn't care as long as no swans had their beady eyes on him. Having finally lost them, a relieved Henry turned onto his street only to find seven large white swans blocking his way. They stared at him and he stared at them for a long moment, like rival cowboys in a lawless town in the old American Wild West.

"Shoo!..." Henry flapped his hands futilely at them. "Shoo! Go away!"

This was not at all like a cowboy in a lawless town in the old American Wild West. It's unlikely any cowboy ever shouted "shoo!" at his rivals and flapped his arms in an erratic manner in the hope of disbursing them. And if one did, he more than likely got shot. This *not* being the lawless American Wild West, Henry did not get shot. But he also did not disburse these determined swans.

Henry thought about what his options might be, but his course of action was decided for him when he saw the sergeant from the police station driving down the street in a black-and-white. Worried the cop would spot him and give him another fine for having swans—or worse, lock him up pending a psychiatric evaluation—Henry felt forced to quickly guide all seven swans up the front porch steps and into his house. Slamming the door behind him, he stood there wondering what to do next.

At this point, the largest swan stepped forward, opened his beak, and honked several times at Henry. If you've ever heard a swan honk, you'll know that it sounds like an old-fashioned car horn. The type with a squeezy ball attached to a large brass horn that makes a two-note honking sound as air is squeezed out and then drawn back in again. In this instance, however, Henry would have sworn that the swan honked the words *true love... true love, true love.*

Chapter 34

STANDING IN THE entrance hall listening to the swan honk at him, Henry felt a very strange sensation. Fear? Panic? Confusion? No. Actually, yes, he felt all those things. But he *also* felt...

Wind.

Not "wind," like he had gas and was about to fart. Grow up... although... that would be pretty funny.

No, he felt normal wind. Like a breeze. Only, it wasn't *normal* because there shouldn't be a breeze *inside* the hallway of his house. He bravely pushed past the swans blocking his way and walked to the back of the house, where he found the source of the wind.

The back door was open. The door to

the garden. The door to Katie's garden. The door to Katie's garden that he had locked shut with a dead bolt and instructions that it never be opened. And yet, there it was. Open.

He stood in the doorway at the top of the four iron steps, overgrown with weeds and vines, that led down into the garden, where he saw the six geese from the previous day happily and quietly feasting on leaves, foliage, and grasses.

"What are you doing?" Henry asked, staring at Will and Ella, who froze at the sound of his voice as if caught in the middle of some devious act rather than standing in the garden of their own house enjoying a bit of nature.

"It's not their fault, Mr. Sullivan. It was me," said Mariana in her quick-fire Hispanic lilt. "They told me not to open the back door. They told me not to let the geese into the garden. But they were hungry—the geese, not your children, although maybe your children, too. You know you have no fresh food in your house at all, which can't be good for growing children, who need fruit and vegetables that are not frozen or canned. I mean, powdered milk is one thing, but—"

"My God, stop speaking," Henry instructed.

At this point, Will and Ella stepped in to explain that they had called Mariana after Will was nearly pecked to death having attempted to retrieve his toothbrush from the geese's bathroom. Unfortunately, in his haste to escape, he neglected to shut the door securely, so the geese burst from their confinement and stormed the house like particularly petulant Visigoths attacking the Roman empire.

If the geese were unpleasant before confinement, they were positively rabid after twelve hours locked in a bathroom. They ran riot around the house, pecking and nipping at Will and Ella, who fended them off as best they could with brooms and mops. But with dwindling energy and facing a superior foe, Ella felt forced to call in reinforcements in the form of Mariana, who mercifully arrived within minutes as she happened to live very close by.

"The geese were simply hungry," Mariana explained to Henry. "They eat roots, grasses,

bulbs, small insects…so I suggested the garden would be the natural place for them."

"This garden is off-limits," said Henry definitively, waving an authoritarian finger in
the air. "It is not for geese. Or people. Or any
other animals for that matter."

As if to specifically contradict him, the seven
swans meandered out past him and made
themselves entirely at home in an ornamental
stone fountain full of rainwater. The fountain
had been largely hidden by foliage, but the
geese had done a good job of pulling back the
vines that covered it.

Katie had found the fountain in a salvage
yard in New Jersey. The owner of the vast
basin had told them a long, involved story
about it having been the centerpiece of a grand
mansion built in the 1890s as a wedding
present for a railroad heiress whose marriage
sadly never took place because the groom
died unexpectedly of a particularly aggressive
case of restless leg syndrome. The seller had
acquired the fountain when the crumbling,
neglected mansion was pulled down.

Softened by Katie's enthusiasm for the

romance of the piece, he allowed Henry to buy it for a knockdown price. Only after buying it did Henry learn that the delivery price of the hulking mass of granite would be ten times the purchase price. The look on Katie's face, however, when it was finally installed, was worth every penny to Henry.

"What...are *those*?" asked Ella tentatively, pointing at the swans.

"What do you mean, '*what are those*'? I would've thought it's pretty damn clear what they are. But let's see if we can figure this out together," Henry mused sarcastically. "Hm...white, feathery, web-footed, swan-necked...I've got it! They're elephants!"

"Okay, Dad. Calm down. I was only asking," said Ella.

"Sorry." A defeated Henry exhaled. "Swans. Seven of them."

"Just like the..." Will whispered.

"Don't say it. Just don't say it," responded Henry. "It was like they hunted me down."

"They're a-swimming," said Mariana with

a bright smile on her face, unaware of the trauma the swans were causing the Sullivans.

"Swimming," Henry corrected.

"Yes, that's what I said: they're a-swimming," Mariana repeated. Because of her Guatemalan accent when speaking English, Mariana often put an "a" sound in front of words beginning with consonants. "How beautiful. To have in your garden, seven swans a-swimming," she repeated.

"And six geese a-laying," Ella added, nodding toward the geese, who seemed to produce eggs ceaselessly.

"Five golden rings," Will smiled.

"Four calling birds," huffed Henry.

"Three French hens," remembered Mariana.

"Two turtle doves," said Henry.

"And a partridge," smiled Ella, looking down to find Alan pecking on her shoe.

"In this pear tree," said Will, carrying the potted tree out of the house and setting it down on the ground in the garden.

The three Sullivans shared a chuckle, marveling for a moment at the absurdity of all the gifts they had received. They looked at

Mariana, waiting for her to get in on the joke. But she didn't. She looked at them staring at her.

"What?" she asked.

"The song," Ella urged.

But Mariana just shrugged. Having grown up in Guatemala, she was blissfully unaware of the Christmas carol that Ms. Truelove was following. If she had heard the carol during the two years she had lived in Austin as a little girl, she had forgotten it. Just like she had forgotten other things that seemed so important from her time in America like the names of her Bratz dolls and the rules of Candy Land.

"Never mind," said Henry. "It's nothing." He decided that it was probably a good thing that Mariana didn't know what was going on. It would only have provoked more questions that they couldn't answer. At least not in English, apparently. So, expecting the worst, Henry just asked, "With all these new birds, I suppose you're going to give me more fines?"

"Actually, by keeping them in this garden, you have adequate room and food for the geese and swans so I don't think you are contravening any city ordinances," Mariana said, softly smiling. "They are migratory birds and if they choose to settle for a while in your garden, then so be it."

The Sullivans breathed a collective sigh of relief. Possibly the first piece of good news they'd received in a week.

"Just don't get a tiger." Mariana laughed.

Fear flashed in the eyes of all three Sullivans. Although Mariana was joking, a tiger was a distinct possibility for the next gift from the mysterious, deranged, nutcase Ms. Truelove. But then they collectively realized that swans had to be the last gift she'd send. In the carol, "The Twelve Days of Christmas," after swans, it's maids. And, looking at the increasingly shabby state of their house, it would be out of character for Ms. Truelove to send anything near as useful as eight maids.

"Does anyone here like hot chocolate?" Mariana asked, unzipping her backpack and pulling out a brightly colored canister. "This morning, I received from home the finest cocoa powder in the world. Made from

Guatemalan cacao, of course. You guys look like you could use some Christmas cheer."

Will and Ella's faces had brightened at the thought of hot chocolate, but they looked nervously toward their father at the mention of taboo "Christmas cheer."

Henry sniffed, then said, "Sure, some 'cheer' would be nice," deliberately leaving out the word *Christmas.*

"But," Mariana looked at Henry and said seriously, "we will need milk. *Real* milk. Not powdered."

He smiled. "I'll go get some."

With everyone back inside, Henry turned around to close the door to the garden. Reaching up to slide the heavy dead bolt back across the doorframe, he paused to look outside once more at the garden now being enjoyed by the geese and swans. He withdrew his hand, deciding that maybe it would be okay to leave the door unbolted. For the moment anyway.

On the Eighth Day

Chapter 35

IT WAS JUST as well that Henry left the back
door unbolted, as the geese were restless.
While the swans were perfectly happy to stay
in the garden, the geese, on the other hand,
liked to come and go.

So, throughout the night, the Sullivans
were awoken by insistent pecking on the
inside or outside of the back door, depend-
ing on whether the geese were outside and
wanted to be let in or were inside and wanted
to be let out. When definitively woken at
6:42 a.m.—as they had been every morning since the calling birds had arrived four
days prior—the Sullivans were forced to walk
through a newly laid minefield of goose eggs
to get to anywhere in the house. Bleary-eyed

after a fitful night's sleep, the first task for each of the Sullivans that morning was to clean yolk and eggshell from between their toes and to wipe up eggy messes from the carpets or floorboards.

Ms. Truelove hadn't just sent any old geese. In her strict adherence to the rules of the song, she had very specifically sent *geese a-laying.*

When Ella had first seen the huge stacks of egg cartons in the back of the SUV, she'd assumed it was a lifetime supply. Not so. It had only been two days and they were nearly full. The geese were relentless. Cartons full of goose eggs were stacked up, lining the hallways all around the house.

Dodging and gathering eggs, Will and Ella went about their new morning chores with admirable and resigned efficiency. The birds were duly fed, watered, mucked out, and tended as necessary. Ella was in more of a hurry than Will, as she had to scrub herself clean and get to school. Will, now suspended, had the luxury of time, but he also had the burden of extra chores.

"Where's Alan?" Will asked Ella, pointing to the partridge's empty shoebox.

Ella didn't know. Nor did Henry. Worryingly, nobody had seen the little partridge chick that morning. This revelation led to an increasingly frantic search of the house, including all coat pockets, which did not produce the chick. He (or she) was nowhere to be found. And each of the Sullivans was secretly surprised by feeling a deep sense of worry for the tiny, frail chick. Not that they would admit it to each other, but each had, for their own reasons, grown quite fond of the little guy (or girl).

"Look," said Will, pointing at a window. It was open a crack and a couple of small, downy feathers were stuck to the sill. "Who opened the window?"

Ella sheepishly admitted she did. The smell of wildlife had grown pretty overwhelming to her. "I only opened it an inch. I didn't think Alan would squeeze out." Ella was torn. On the one hand, she felt guilty and wanted to go look for him (or her). On the other hand, she had promised Suzanne they would get started on the new *blue* designs for the musical back-drops before classes started. "I feel terrible, but I really have to get to school now."

"And I have a ton of essays to grade before my first lecture," said Henry, gesturing toward a stack of papers on the table.

"It's okay," said Will, surprising his father and sister by taking responsibility. "You guys do what you need to do. I'll find Alan."

Chapter 36

ONCE SUITABLY INSULATED against the cold, Will stepped out into the street. It had rained again that night, so Will was thankfully able to follow tiny, wet partridge footprints on the gray paving stones. As he followed the trail like some kind of pet detective in search of his missing client, Will wondered if Ms. Truelove had any idea how absurd she had made his life. He wondered who she could be and whether she was keeping an eye on them somehow, laughing at how they were being driven nuts.

The footprints took him up to 127th Street but had begun getting fainter and farther apart as puddles dried up in the morning sun. Will needed to follow faster or the footprints would entirely disappear and, with them, any chance of rescuing Alan from the one million ways a partridge chick might die on the island of Manhattan.

Looking around for help, Will spotted a bicycle—not locked or anything—leaning up against a wall. You never see an unlocked bicycle in Manhattan. And, yet, here one was. And not any bicycle. A child-size bicycle perfect for someone Will's height. It was as if it had been gifted to him by divine providence in his hour of need. Of course, Will knew that stealing was wrong. He had learned that lesson pretty thoroughly just two days ago. But *borrowing*—especially in the pursuit of such a noble life-saving cause—must be acceptable, right? And, besides, Will could return it to the exact same spot when done. In no more than an hour. It probably wouldn't even be missed. And, if it was, it would be nothing less than a well-needed lesson in responsibility for the careless owner.

So Will casually took hold of the handlebars, swung a leg over the saddle, and pedaled like the wind in the direction the partridge footprints were leading him. Five frantic minutes later he came to the end of the trail, discovering the little fellow standing outside a house on a quiet, tree-lined residential street.

"There you are, Alan," Will said, scooping the chick up in his hands and holding it up to his face. "Decided to stretch your legs, did you? You gave us quite a scare."

"Who are you t-t-t-talking to?"

"Nobody!" Will said, shoving the chick quickly into his pocket, as if talking to nobody was somehow less nuts than talking to a partridge chick. Will looked around to see Benny standing in the doorway of the house Alan had randomly decided to lead him to. "What are you doing here?"

"I l-l-live here. We m-moved a couple years ago."

"Oh. Nice." Will nodded approvingly, ignoring the twinge of guilt he felt for being so ignorant of his former best friend's life.

"W-what are you doing here?" Benny asked.

"Uuuuuhhhhhh, just out for a cycle ride," said Will, which although not a lie, was not the entire truth.

"Want to c-come in?" Benny offered.

Will didn't. But he *was* quite cold and *did* need to pee. So Will followed Benny inside, marveling at the cozy, bright, orderly rooms, which were quite a contrast to those of his home. Even better, the bathroom was delightfully free of geese, so, for the first time in a couple days, Will could take his time to do his business without fear of a goose attack. Suitably relieved, Will eventually settled into the warm kitchen while Benny made them toast with a thick layer of lustrous apple butter.

"I heard you got sus-s-spended," Benny said. "Did you tell Mr. Fitzatelli who m-made you do it?"

"They didn't *make me* do it," Will corrected. "I did it 'cause I wanted to. And, anyway, you don't tattle on your friends, Benny."

"*F-f-f-friends?!* They left you to take the blame! They r-ran away!"

"You wouldn't understand," said Will, repeating the motto of people who know they're wrong, but are too proud to admit it. Deep down, however, it did bother Will that none of his "posse" had come by, or even called, to check on him. But he was sure they had their reasons. Well, not *sure*. But *assumed* they had their reasons. He certainly *wanted to believe* they had their reasons. At the very least, he *hoped* they had good reasons for not checking on him.

"I gotta g-get to school," said Benny, pulling on his coat.

"You have a bike? I'll bike there with you," Will offered.

"I c-can't."

"Oh, what? You can't be seen with me? 'Cause I'm suspended?" Will chided. "Is that what it is? Wow. And *you* were lecturing *me* about friends."

"No. I m-mean, I can't r-ride a bike. Never learned," corrected Benny.

"What?!" Will laughed. "You never learned to ride a bike? Come on, man, like, five-year-old kids can ride bikes."

Benny looked down at his shoes as Will continued to laugh.

"I never l-learned, okay!" Benny said angrily. "M-my dad never had time to t-teach me. So I can't!"

"All right, all right. Calm down," said Will, remembering that Benny's dad wasn't around much.

"Y-you've changed," Benny said quietly, opening the front door for Will.

"And you haven't," said Will in the way that people who are hurt try to hurt others back.

Chapter 37

WILL HAD PROMISED that he'd return the stolen bike immediately after finding Alan. But, since he'd made that promise, it had started drizzling and the temperature had dropped. If he returned it now, the chick would get wet and cold. So, reasoning that he could easily return the bike tomorrow, he headed straight home, scheming how to hide the bike from his father.

The last thing Will needed was to be interrogated by Henry about the sudden appearance of a shiny new bike. At least, he *thought* that was the last thing he needed. But that was *not* the last thing Will needed. The last thing he needed, he would soon learn, was in fact...cows.

As Will pedaled onto his own street, he was immediately enveloped by bovine-induced pandemonium. A long line of frustrated drivers honking their car horns were at a standstill as a small herd of fifteen-hundred-pound black-and-white heifers blocked the road directly in front of Will's house. Moos and honks mingled with insults and demands shouted by angry drivers leaning out of car windows.

In the middle of it all was Henry trying to communicate with several robust, blond pigtailed women. Each woman wore a different-colored variation on the traditional German dirndl outfit that consisted of voluminous petticoats under a skirt with an apron and a tightly laced-up bodice over an extravagantly ruffled white shirt. In short, their clothing was entirely out of place in a modern American urban environment. Most of these women were seated on wooden stools near the rear of a cow, pulling industriously on udders, seemingly oblivious to the havoc around them. Will counted the women and counted the cows.

"Oh...my...God," he muttered dumbly. "Eight maids a-milking!"

As he approached, Will saw his father attempting to restore order. He was hampered by the fact that the German women spoke no English. And, in case you hadn't already figured it out, Henry spoke no German.

Henry slowly shouted at one of them, "You cannot stay here."

She simply responded with one word. "Sullivan?"

"Yes?" Henry answered, surprised that she knew his name.

She just smiled and shouted to her compatriots, *"Ja! Das ist es!!"*

"No!" Henry responded, correctly guessing the gist of what she said. *"Das ist* DEFINITELY NOT *es. Nein nein!* NOT *es* at all!!"

But they did not listen. One by one, the milkmaids kissed Henry on both cheeks, exclaiming "Herr Sullivan!" and then bear-hugging him forcefully enough to squeeze the air out of his lungs with an elongated wheeze.

Taking advantage of the commotion, Will

safely stashed the stolen bike behind a bush before approaching his red-faced father.

A driver shouted above the hubbub, "Get your girlfriends out of the street!"

Wriggling out of the grasp of the last milk-maid, Henry responded, "These ladies are NOT my girlfriends!"

"I was talking about the cows!" shouted the driver back, raising a laugh from the other drivers. Say what you like about New Yorkers, but they never lose their sense of humor, even in the most disturbing of situations. Henry, by the way, was not a native New Yorker and had definitely lost his sense of humor.

"Dad!" said Will, pulling Henry back. "Get them into the garden!"

Faced with no other option, Henry and Will herded the milkmaids and their cows down the narrow alley alongside the house. There, Henry spun the numbered disks on the gate padlock toward the date of Katie's birthday and unlatched it.

Ushering the livestock and milkmaids in, Henry heard the beeping and shouting die down to be replaced by purring engines and free-flowing traffic.

"Henry," said Mr. Greenblatt, the neighbor, leaning out of his upstairs window and pointing to several hub-cap-size cow poops that lay steaming in the alley, "I don't want to hear you complain about my dog ever again."

A moment later, Henry and Will stood in the kitchen, looking through the window into the garden. The eight milkmaids busily milked their eight cows as if a Harlem backyard was as natural a place for them as a Tyrolean hilltop.

"She sent us...cows," said Henry numbly.

"Forget the cows, Dad. She sent us *people*," responded Will.

There was no doubt that they were from *her*. Stitching on each milkmaid's dirndl read *Wahre Liebe Milchbauernhof*, which the computer translated to *True Love Dairies*. But, interestingly, none of the internet-connected devices in the house would translate *anything else* into or out of German no matter how hard or how often they pressed Return.

"What are we going to do?" Will asked.

"I don't know about you, Will, but I have to go to work," said Henry, turning and walking away.

Will rushed after him. "You can't leave me here."

"Someone needs to stay to look after everything. If you had school, maybe I'd stay instead. But since you got yourself suspended, well...you're in charge."

As Henry opened the front door, they heard a crashing, sploshing sound behind them. One of the milkmaids had spilled an entire bucket of milk, creating a white mini-wave along the wood floorboards of the hallway.

"Entschuldigung," she said with an apologetic curtsy.

"I assume that means 'there's a mop in the closet,'" said Henry dryly, leaving the house. As he closed the door after him, he snuck a satisfactory look at the fear in Will's eyes. *Every cloud has a silver lining,* thought Henry.

Chapter 38

HENRY'S CONTENTED SATISFACTION was short-lived.

It lasted through his first class, a coffee break, and the subsequent stroll to his office. But it was entirely shattered when his friend Dr. Fringe appeared in the doorway. Despite Henry's strange behavior the previous day, Dr. Fringe seemed unconcerned, and Henry took some comfort in his friend's good-natured trust in him. The conversation started encouragingly enough...

"I have good news!" Dr. Fringe announced as he dropped heavily into a comfy chair, creating a puff of dust divinely illuminated by the low winter sun's streaming in through the window behind him.

"Oh?" Henry said. "Do go on."

Had Henry known what was to come, he wouldn't have said, "Do go on." He probably would have covered his ears and loudly said something like "Blah blah blah I can't hear you blah blah blah." But since he didn't, Dr. Fringe went on as invited.

"I've spoken to Dean Grumpf and I think we have a solution. We need to help him see what a good man you are. A family man. With responsibilities. A man who needs this job and can rise to the occasion. That way, we can win him over and change his mind."

"Sounds great. What's the plan?"

"Dinner at your house." Dr. Fringe smiled.

"No! No. No no no no no no no no no...no," said Henry, thinking of the bird/ cow/milkmaid sanctuary that was currently his abode. There was no way that he could entertain at home. Especially if the evil-minded Ms. Truelove planned on continuing with her cruel scheme to fill the house with the gifts from the carol "The Twelve Days of Christmas." How could Henry explain away the presence of milkmaids and whatever came next? Henry struggled to find a way out, and the look on his face betrayed his inner panic.

"Come now," said Fringe, "it's exactly what the situation requires. You used to host wonderful dinners."

"That was...when I had Katie."

This was true. For a moment, Henry allowed himself to think back to all the spur-of-the-moment dinners they'd hosted, where Katie would somehow whip up the most amazing delicacies out of whatever happened to be in the cupboards or in the garden. She'd then set the table in an imaginative way, using pine cones or artichokes as decoration. And she'd keep the conversation flowing, making everyone feel at ease. In short, she did everything so Henry could simply be relaxed and charming. He was neither of those things without her.

"No," Henry implored. "It can't be done. The house is a mess."

"I'm sure it's not that bad." Dr. Fringe laughed.

"No. It *really* is. We cannot have dinner at my house."

Dr. Fringe leaned forward and looked

seriously at Henry. "I'm doing my best to help you, yet it feels like you're fighting me every step of the way. Although still hell-bent on getting rid of you, Dean Grumpf was willing to give you this one last opportunity. So it's this or nothing."

Dr. Fringe stood up with the prolonged groan of a large and overweight man. "In the meantime, I need you to prove to both Dean Grumpf *and me* that you are taking your professorial responsibilities seriously. And that means being on time for all lectures, attending office hours, being available for one-on-one student sessions, and rereading—and I mean *properly* reading—every paper and every exam that your students have written this year and giving them the grades they deserve."

Fringe pulled two tall stacks of papers from his oversize shoulder bag and dropped them onto Henry's desk. *Thud. Thud.*

The sound of the stacks hitting the desk could just as easily have been the sound of Henry's spirits and hope hitting rock bottom.

Chapter 39

IF HENRY AND Will were both overwhelm-
ingly concerned by how they were going to
manage the sudden appearance of eight hearty
German dairy farm technicians and their
eight three-quarter-ton bovine accomplices,
Ella was not worried in the least.

The first reason was that she had enough
worries of her own. The design and execution
of the new blue musical sets was not going
well. She had heard several cast members
questioning the new direction, and Ella didn't
disagree. But there was nothing she could do
except finish them as best she could or face the
wrath of Sally Kensington, who—as opening
night approached—was only becoming more
demanding and imperious.

James Patterson

The second reason that Ella was not worried about the impact of cows and milkmaids was that she *didn't know* about the German invasion that had taken place. When she left for school that morning, the house was an entirely cow-free zone. Arriving home that evening, however, she joined her brother in his general state of freaked-outness amplified by her strong conviction that bovine spongiform encephalopathy (better known as mad cow disease) was sure to have already spread rampantly throughout the house.

"There is a plus side, though," said Will, gesturing to the rows of milk-filled buckets. "Fresh milk is delicious."

"Is it?" asked Ella, breathing through a handkerchief pressed against her mouth.

"No! I was being sarcastic. It's lukewarm, smells like feet, and has things I don't even want to think about floating in it!"

"Hello!" a voice said behind them.

Ella turned to see Mariana coming down the stairs.

"Everything is fine," said Mariana, assuring Will that he would have managed perfectly well without her. The cows were in need of hay and straw. The birds were getting low on feed. But other than that, they were doing very well.

Ella accompanied Will and Mariana out to the garden, which, for five years, had been so dark and still, but was now full of activity with geese, swans, cows, and milkmaids. Grazing cows tearing at the grass had revealed the old stepping-stone paths as well as flower beds, the herb garden, and a vegetable patch. Long-forgotten memories of planting seeds and digging dirt with their mother stirred in both children. Especially when they smelled the unmistakable odor of "fertilizer" that the cows were generously depositing throughout.

"And your father has a problem with the smell of my cooking?!" shouted Mrs. Singh, their neighbor, leaning out of her window and pinching her nose. "Those cows are disgusting. This is NOT legal!"

"Actually," Mariana explained, "there's a Harlem city ordinance from 1762, still on the books, that allows citizens to graze up to ten cows on their land."

"There is?"

Mariana did a combination nod and shrug, which gives the impression of being apologetic when you really don't feel sorry at all.

"Well, it's not nice!" said Mrs. Singh, slamming her window shut.

"Lucky you knew about that law." Ella nodded, impressed.

"I made it up." Mariana smiled. "But, seriously, why in the world are there eight cows and eight German milkmaids here?"

Will and Ella stammered for an answer, but luckily the phone rang and they both dashed inside. It was their father, sounding exhausted, informing them that he had a ton of work and would be back late. But he wanted to make sure that everything was under control at home.

Will and Ella looked around. Everything was indeed under control... in that the entire house was fully under the control of the laws of chaos. There were French hens locked in a turf battle with the turtle doves over living room real estate. The geese were pecking the sofa cushions to death, sending flurries of feathers and stuffing into the air. Two swans were hissing at a milkmaid who was attempting to get to the bathroom. There were at least twenty-eight buckets of milk lined up on the sides of the hallway. Ella counted twelve smashed goose eggs on the floor. And a cow had wandered into the kitchen, where she had apparently decided that the floor tiles needed to be fertilized.

"We're…absolutely fine, Dad. You do what you need to do," Ella said and hung up.

"We're *fine*?" asked Will incredulously. "There's a cow in the kitchen."

"He needs us to be fine. And we will be."

After Mariana helped them push the cow back into the garden, she had to go to work but said that she'd expect a full explanation. They lied that all would be revealed next time they saw her.

Now alone, Ella turned to Will. "Come on. We have work to do."

"Where do we even start?" Will sighed.

"If you take care of the birds, I'll take care of dinner."

"Dinner? How? We never have enough food

in the house for the three of *us*. Forget feeding eight strangers who honestly look like they could strip an all-you-can-eat buffet in sixty seconds."

"Will…we have an *endless* supply of food in the house," said Ella, holding up a goose egg. "Omelet, anyone?"

Chapter 40

AT THE END of the night, Ella rubbed her aching right arm and shoulder, trying to unknot the tight muscles and throbbing joints. Over the past two hours, at her best estimate, she had beaten *seventy* goose eggs to make omelets for the voracious milkmaids, who ploughed through them like they hadn't eaten all day...which was fair because they hadn't. No sooner had Ella served eggs to the last milkmaid than the first one was standing in front of her again with an empty plate and a big smile, saying, *"mehr bitte,"* which Ella guessed correctly meant "more, please." And so the chain went on for several hours.

Will had lived up to his part of the bargain, efficiently taking care of the birds' bedtime routines. So by the end of the night, after an exhausted, sore, slow-moving Ella had finished cleaning and disinfecting the kitchen, things in the Sullivan household looked fairly normal. Not *normal* normal. Just the *normal* that you could expect from an urban townhouse that was home to twenty-three birds, eight cows, and eight stocky blond-pigtailed German ladies.

Sure, there were still buckets of milk everywhere, cartons of goose eggs piled up, a certain amount of destruction to the soft furnishings, and considerable staining to the carpets... but, all in all, things were largely in hand. Ella finally felt she could retire to her room.

Never had the thought of a warm cozy bed been more welcome. But Ella opened the door to her bedroom—her sanctuary—to see her worst nightmare. Well, not her *worst* nightmare, in that there was not a seven-foot-tall, clawed E. coli monster made up of millions of other tiny, writhing bacteria trying to lick her. But this was pretty close.

Inside her bedroom, all eight milkmaids

were spread out, having entirely made themselves at home among Ella's dearest and formerly cleanest possessions. One maid had her bare foot up on Ella's chest of drawers to cut her toenails, the clippings flying off to be lost in the deep pile of the carpet. Another was using Ella's face washcloth to scrub her armpits! Several had squeezed themselves into Ella's pristine pajamas. And, worst of all, one was brushing her teeth with Ella's electric toothbrush.

When the milkmaids saw her in the doorway, however, they grabbed Ella—paralyzed by shock—and pulled her into the room like this was a prearranged sleepover that Ella had spearheaded. She could only smile numbly as they took turns hugging her limp body like a communal rag doll. Ella did not like physical contact at the best of times. And this was as far from the best of times as she could imagine.

Without any alternative, Ella stayed in the room and, avoiding physical contact as much as possible, found and changed into her last remaining clean pair of pajamas. Then, having brushed her teeth using her finger, she slid into bed between three slumbering milkmaids. The others were variously snoring loudly under her desk, in her chair, or curled up on cushions on the floor.

Ella lay stiff as a board with one milkmaid's bottom firmly pressed into her thigh and another drooling slowly onto her shoulder. Faced with the impossibility of sleep, Ella reached for her laptop and her headphones and began surfing the internet.

On the Ninth Day

Chapter 41

THE NEXT MORNING, a tired Henry made his way downstairs, weaving between goose eggs and buckets of milk, past the living room where the calling birds were pecking at his library—everyone's a critic—and the French hens were sitting on the sofa watching *Good Morning America*. The previous night, he had stayed late in his dusty office on campus and arrived home only after everyone else was asleep.

In the kitchen, he found Ella, looking every bit as tired as he did. She handed her surprised father a mug of hot coffee. He was surprised because she had never in all her life made him a cup of coffee. All the same, he took a sip and was immediately struck by the intense, velvety, warm deliciousness.

"Honey, that's amazing. I really appreciate it, but you can't just go out and buy expensive imported coffee. We're on a tight budget—"

"Dad," she stopped him, "it's not new coffee. It's new *milk*. Very new. In fact, it was inside that cow an hour ago."

With a grimace, Henry let a mouthful of coffee dribble back into the mug.

"I pasteurized it," Ella reassured him, pointing to pots double-boiling on the stove with a large thermometer sticking out of the top one. This is what she had stayed up late researching on the internet: how to make use of the gallons of milk that were being produced by the cows in the garden every day.

Henry looked at her. "Are you *sure* this is safe?"

"Have you met me?" Ella asked sarcastically, taking a sip of fresh milk cooling on the table. "Of course it's safe."

"We'll find out in about four hours if it's not," he said, enjoying another large gulp of his delicious coffee.

"You won't want this then," Ella said, presenting him with a fresh-from-the-pan glistening, steaming omelet. "Goose eggs," she explained.

"*You* made this?" Henry said, impressed by the daughter he didn't think knew one end of a wooden spoon from the other. He took a bite and his eyes nearly rolled back in his head in culinary ecstasy. "Holy crap. Are those chives in there?"

"Turns out, there are a bunch of herbs still growing in Mom's herb garden. Chives, mint, rosemary, thyme, oregano, and a couple others."

"That's amazing. Mom always did say herbs were weeds and nearly impossible to kill." Henry's mind conjured a clear memory of Katie cutting and gathering herbs for dinner.

"Yeah," agreed Ella, picturing the same image before adding, "Mariana found them yesterday."

Henry's ears pricked up. "Mariana was here? You called her?"

"I didn't call her, no. I thought you must've

called her to check up on Will. I guess he felt overwhelmed and called her himself."

"Hm." Henry nodded, munching absently on his omelet, seemingly lost in his own thoughts. "Interesting."

"What's interesting?" asked Ella bluntly, never having seen her father mentally drift off like that.

"Oh. Well…uh, that she found fresh spices," he responded. "They might come in handy because…" He paused. "…we're having Provost Fringe and Dean Grumpf over for dinner the night after tomorrow."

"Here?!"

"Yes."

"In *this* house? The house we're standing in. The house filled with aquatic birdlife, farm animals, and non-English-speaking total strangers who have no reason to be here whatsoever?"

"Yes."

"They'll think we're insane."

"You don't think I tried to stop it? It's unavoidable if I'm to keep my job. Which I'd like to do. Unless, of course, you no longer want to live in a house…or eat food…or wear clothes."

Ella admitted that she did indeed still want those things. But before they could discuss the matter further, the milkmaids began filing into the kitchen.

"*Gutentag,* Herr Sullivan!" They cheerfully nodded one after the next.

"Yes, yes, *gutentag* to you, too," he said glumly. "How are you all enjoying living rent-free in my house, eating my food, and…wearing my slippers?"

Confronted by eight expectant milkmaids looking at her hungrily, Ella, although beyond exhausted, picked up a fork, swung her arm around a couple of times to warm it up, and then, with impressive speed and ferocity, began to beat a great and heavy quantity of goose eggs in a very large glass bowl.

The goose eggs, however, were not the only ones facing a beating…

Chapter 42

As ELLA AND Henry sat in the kitchen, Will had cycled that morning to the pet store to restock supplies for the birds. He was on his return journey, pedaling toward home, when he heard a commanding, manly, *Swedish* voice shout out.

"Halt, you thieving lowlife brigand!"

Will looked around, excited by the prospect of possibly witnessing a bank robbery. Maybe a shootout. Or a car chase. But he was disappointed to realize that the "thieving lowlife brigand" was in fact...himself.

There are 146,309 people (give or take a few) who live in Harlem. If the bike Will stole had belonged to any of 146,308 of them, Will would have been okay. But there was one person he really didn't want the bike to belong to. And that person was the notoriously strong, notoriously noble, notoriously *punishing* Swedish demigod among middle schoolers, Gus Gustavson. And for those of you who are a little slower to pick up on these things...that was who the bike belonged to.

As a sixth grader, Gus had famously beaten Mr. Fitzatelli at arm wrestling. And Mr. Fitzatelli was no lanky, pencil-necked geek. He had played professional football for two years (albeit in the Canadian league, but still...).

In a single stomach-shrinking moment, all moisture in Will's mouth evaporated, relocating to the palms of his hands.

"Hi, Gus." Will smiled weakly. "Is this *yours*? I thought it was mine."

"Really?" said Gus, who liked to believe in the innate goodness of people.

"Yeah, I mean, all kids' bikes look alike. Handlebars, wheels, seat..."

"Except this is a one-of-a-kind, custom-built bike from when I was the under-fifteen

Swedish BMX champion of Ostergotland. Painted in my racing colors. And engraved with my initials."

Will removed his hands from the handlebars and there indeed, as promised, were the initials "G.G." as clear as day.

"Um, well, I see the error of my ways," said Will, stepping off the bike and pushing it toward Gus, who towered a good six inches over him. "I apologize sincerely. I'll be on my way now."

Gus stopped him. "You think you can commit a crime and not receive a punishment for it?"

Will swallowed hard. "Punishment? What sort of punishment?"

"We fight!" Gus said matter-of-factly.

"Now?" Will asked in what was pretty close to a whimper.

"No...I'm late for rehearsal. And I don't want to feel rushed."

"Wouldn't want that," said Will, his sarcasm lost on Gus.

"Thank you." Gus thought for a moment before declaring, "No, we'll do it right before the opening night of the musical. The adrenaline rush will boost my performance. Shall we say the alley behind school, 2:30 p.m., Christmas Eve?"

Will swallowed hard. All his powers of charm and persuasion seemed to abandon him. But then, as a stroke of magnificent luck, he saw his posse strolling around the corner. Even with the sun behind them, casting them into four silhouettes, Will could clearly make out the unmistakable hunched, loping outlines of Cuz, Noodle, Bean, and Fash! Emboldened by their arrival, Will straightened up and smiled.

"You just try to beat me up," taunted Will, adding loudly enough for his pals to hear, "you big, stupid Swedish meatball."

"You are *insulting* me?" puzzled the Swede. "You know this only makes me more angry and determined to pummel you for stealing my bike?"

Will smiled. "But that is not going to happen, is it, guys? ... Guys?"

"You stole his bike?" Cuz asked incredulously.

"That's not cool, man," added Fash.

"You guys steal all the time," pointed out a confused Will.

"Not from *people*," said Noodle. "From shops. It's a victimless crime."

"I'm kind of disappointed in you," added Cuz.

"We're getting off point—I think—" Will stammered. "We can discuss the ethics of stealing later. Let's focus on the part where he wants to beat the crap out of me."

"What about it?" asked Fash.

"You're not going to let him do that, are you?" prompted Will.

"I feel this is between you and him," said Bean. "We'll stay out of it."

"You'll *stay out of it*? You can't *stay out of it*. I got caught stealing exams for you!" Will strongly reminded them. "I got *suspended* for you! I nearly fell from a second-story window!"

"In hindsight," shrugged Noodle, "that was stupid, dude. You probably shouldn't have done that. See ya 'round."

On that note, they walked away, speculating

casually about which of Will's bones Gus would break first. Leaving Will to wonder if there was a boarding school in Timbuktu that might be accepting student applications.

Chapter 43

NORMALLY, AFTER SCHOOL, Ella would go straight upstairs and closet herself in her room to do some solitary activity, like painting, drawing, or disinfecting. But since the milkmaids had taken up permanent residence in her sanctuary, Ella was forced to remain downstairs. And since the birds had taken over the living room and dining room, Ella wound up in the kitchen. And if she was going to be stuck in the kitchen, she might as well have a look around and explore the cabinets.

For five years, there had not been any real cooking in the house. There had been plenty of *defrosting, boiling, microwaving, unwrapping, toasting, heating up,* and *just-add-water-ing.* But no actual *cooking.* Until now.

Ella once again began dinner preparations, cracking goose eggs into a bowl and beating them. What was exhausting and messy just a day ago was relatively effortless today. And, having found her mother's old handwritten recipe cards at the back of a cupboard, she was looking forward to making cheese and herb frittatas for everyone.

Sent off to work that morning with his tail largely bushy and his eyes relatively bright, a depleted Henry arrived home after a full day of lecturing followed by one-on-one tutoring sessions with a parade of his most tedious and pseudo-intellectual students. He poured himself a large Scotch and dropped onto the creaking sofa (between a French hen and a goose), trying his best to enjoy his drink and ignore the range of activities, noises, and smells that were raging around him. It was not easy.

"Hey, Dad," said Will nervously, entering the room. "Can I talk to you?"

"To *me*?" Henry was surprised by the request. "About what? Why? What did you do?" he said, struggling to heave himself out of the sagging sofa.

"I didn't do anything!" insisted Will loudly, hurt that his father automatically went there. "Why would you automatically go there?"

"Will, I'm a history professor," Henry explained. "All of my assumptions about the present are based on what has occurred in the past. So if I ask what you've done wrong now, it's only because of your long history of doing wrong."

"That's not fair," said Will heatedly.

"Fair or not," said a weary Henry, "eighty percent of our conversations are about your misbehavior."

"Whose fault is that?!" Will protested.

"Whose fault is it that you misbehave?" asked Henry pointedly.

"No, whose fault is it that that's the only thing we talk about? There are a million things we could discuss, but you only want to talk about my misbehaving."

"Well, it DOES demand a lot of attention," said Henry, raising his voice to the same level as Will's.

"Maybe I'd misbehave less if we talked more about other things!"

"And we'd have more opportunity to talk about other things if we didn't have to keep talking about your misbehavior!"

Before it could get any more heated, Ella intervened, "Guys, GUYS!..."

She knew about Will's upcoming fight. Everyone at school knew about it. News had spread like butter on a hot pan. There would be a crowd gathered to watch Gus mete out punishment to her brother, the bike thief. She could tell that Will was worried. But before she could intervene, she was distracted by a distant noise. "What's that?"

Will and Henry listened, too. There was music coming from upstairs. Loud, fast-paced orchestra chorus-line music.

"Please tell me you're watching *Moulin Rouge!* in your room, Will," Henry asked hopefully.

"No," replied Will, as puzzled as the others.

Then loud stomping began in time with the music. The living room ceiling shook and the light fixture swung to the rhythm of the stomping.

The Sullivans had all been so wrapped up

in their own problems and chores that they'd somehow forgotten about Ms. Truelove and her gifts.

"Ladies dancing," all three said simultaneously.

Chapter 44

In Will's room, they found nine striking, raven-haired Gallic beauties in a line, wearing red and black ruffled dresses, kicking their feet up high and swinging their fishnet-stocking-clad calves in midair circles. Beside them was an old-fashioned phonograph loudly playing a scratchy record of cancan music. On the record label was clearly written "*Cabaret de L'Amour Vrai,*" or, as Google Translate would soon tell them, "The True Love Cabaret."

"How did you get up here?! Where did you come from?!" shouted Henry.

As with the German milkmaids, however, there was no common form of communication between the Sullivans and the French ladies dancing. In fact, they simply ignored the questions, pulling Will, Ella, and a very reluctant Henry in to join them.

"Let me go!" insisted Henry, extricating himself. "Stop that!"

He yanked Ella and Will out into the hall, leaving the ladies to continue their energetic gyrations. Will left reluctantly, looking over his shoulder, smiling somewhat vacantly at the mesmerizing new inhabitants of his room.

"Ella, go back in and try to get them to stop dancing before the downstairs ceiling falls in. Invite them downstairs for dinner or something. And, Will"—Henry paused, looking ruefully at his son—"they seem to have chosen your room. Like the milkmaids chose Ella's."

"Looks like it," Will concurred.

"I know it's a lot to ask and a terrible imposition, but…are you happy for them to stay in there?"

Will's eyes popped open wide. Had this just gone from being the worst day of the past five years to the best day of the past five years? He swallowed and did his best to answer nonchalantly, "Yeah, sure, if it helps everyone for them to stay in my room, then sure, yeah, I guess I wouldn't mind, you know, in the spirit of generosity and helping out."

"Good," concluded Henry. "They get your room and you can come sleep in my bed with me."

"What!" exclaimed Will. "No. That's not—"

"It's all decided. Excellent. Downstairs for a quick bite. Ella is making something that smells delicious. She is a magician with those goose eggs. Who knew? And then, bedtime. I'm bushed."

On the Tenth Day

Chapter 45

WILL HAD BEEN bushed, too. But he didn't sleep that night. At all.

Yes, he was worried about being pummeled by Gus. Yes, he was disturbed by his friends' betrayal. Yes, he was upset that his father automatically assumed the worst of him. And, yes, he was very distracted by the thought of what the magnificent French dancing ladies might be doing in his room. But none of those things were responsible for keeping him awake that night. There was another, different thought that was devouring him.

How many different, disturbing noises can one man make in his sleep?

This was the question a wide-awake Will kept asking himself as he lay in bed next to his father. The answer that he eventually came up with was: infinite. There seemed to be an infinite number of noises. Snoring, grunting, sniffing, rumbling, clicking, popping, gurgling, nasal whistling, coughing, throat clearing…

At one point, Will was fairly convinced his father was going into labor. But it turned out he was giving birth to nothing more than a monumental sleep-burp…which Will didn't even know was a thing until that moment.

As disturbing as the sounds themselves were the *locations* that they came from. Tummy, mouth, nose, throat, knees, shoulders, and places that Will didn't want to think about. Every now and then, maybe just as Will was beginning to drift off to sleep, he would experience a burst of warm air aimed at his legs under the sheets. And he'd immediately be wide-awake again.

It was with relief that Will heard the calling birds squawking. It was still dark out and he had barely slept at all, but at least Will had an excuse to get out of bed and start his chores.

Chapter 46

HENRY MIGHT HAVE slept incredibly deeply and restoratively that night, but the new day brought him an instant shock that jolted him wide-awake. In his entire adult life, Henry had never had more than one semi-naked woman at a time in his bedroom. In fact, there had been periods of many months at a time when he'd had no women whatsoever in his bedroom. But this morning he woke up to *five*. Wrapped only in towels, two milkmaids and three dancers were waiting in line to go into his en suite bathroom, where a fourth dancer was already in his shower.

This is way too European for me, thought Henry, reaching for whatever clothes were close at hand. He slid them on while still under his sheets before exiting the room at a good pace, his eyes obscured behind a visor made by his hand. While relieved to be out of the naked-strangers situation, downstairs was no less stressful.

Milkmaids trudged back and forth sploshing full buckets of milk into the kitchen. Geese and swans mingled with the other birds making smells and noises while nipping at his shins. Dancing ladies cancanned around them to the constant music playing loudly on the phonograph.

Henry sidestepped the various obstacles until he arrived in the kitchen, where Ella was icing her arm like a postgame quarterback, having whipped possibly a hundred or more goose eggs into omelets for the milkmaids and now the dancing ladies, too. She'd also made Henry another special coffee, for which he thanked her, although his words were barely audible above the general din of the house. She mouthed "you're welcome" before Henry pushed back through the throng and retreated to the relative quiet of the garden. There he sat, bundled in several coats, warming his face over his coffee and enjoying a moment's solitude before he'd have to trudge to work to face the onslaught of eager students. But no sooner had he begun to lose himself in the silky swirls of his coffee than he was nearly hit by something flying over his garden wall and landing by his feet with a thud!

It was an old-fashioned, slightly battered leather suitcase. And embossed in gold into the leather near the brass clasps were initials and a small crown. Then another similar suitcase flew over the wall and landed next to the first. And another and another were lobbed into the garden, scattering whatever geese had been pecking around the area, until eventually ten suitcases lay in a pile on the ground.

"What is going on?" Henry puzzled, reaching down to pick one up.

Before he could, though, he was even more alarmed by a man leaping over the wall and landing acrobatically at his feet with a jolly "Halloooo!" This gentleman was followed by nine more—one by one—leaping over the wall with a "What ho!" or "Pip pip!" or "Ding dong!"

Each man was a distinguished-looking type. Not the sort you'd expect to parkour over your wall in Harlem. Each had a mustache, ranging from the voluminous and droopy to the neatly trimmed. Each was nattily outfitted in a three-piece tweed suit, highly polished brown leather shoes, and regimental-striped tie. Several wore brown felt trilby hats cocked at jaunty angles. And two sported monocles. Following his aerial arrival, each man brushed any dust off his tweed jacket, picked up a suitcase, and started to move inside.

"Whoa whoa whoa! Who the hell are you?" asked Henry, blocking their way.

"Sorry?" responded the first gentleman in a deeply plummy British accent.

"Who the hell are you and what are you doing jumping over my wall?"

The gentleman looked at Henry, puzzled. He turned toward the others, saying, "I believe this rum job is attempting to engage one in a spot of chin-wagging, I daresay. Can any of you chaps fathom the local patois?"

"I'm speaking English," pointed out an

exasperated Henry, his face flushing red. "You're in my garden!"

"Some kind of ballykazzoo far-off dialect," suggested another gentleman to his friends, studying Henry warily through his monocle.

"Step aside, old bean. Let me give it my British best," said a third, pushing his way to the front. He spoke loudly. "I say…we English. Travel far. Stay here."

Henry shouted back, "We're *both* speaking English! And, no, you cannot stay here."

"Nope. It's hopeless. Call Alan Turing. Completely indecipherable." The gent gave up, twirling the left handlebar of his mustache.

"Let's just trot on inside," suggested another.

"Bingo," agreed another. "Check the larder. I've come over all peckish."

"I say, ra-*ther*. Spot of tea, anyone?" recommended a very short, fat one holding up a small brown teapot that was similar in shape to himself.

With that, they pushed past Henry, some handing their hats and coats to their host like he was an obliging butler. They trundled into the house, ignoring Henry's increasingly desperate protests. Hearing the commotion, Ella and Will arrived in the living room only to see the gentlemen making themselves entirely at home. Lounging on the sofa. Reclining in chairs. Two were boiling water on a portable gas cooker. Another unpacked a plate of scones from his suitcase while his friend produced jam and thick, gooey clotted cream.

"Most kind, your lordship," said one, accepting the jam.

"The pleasure's all mine, your lordship."

"Scone, your lordship?"

"Don't mind if I do, your lordship," the short, fat one replied, leaping over the sofa while holding a dainty china teacup with his pinky pointing into the air.

"Ten lords a-leaping, then?" Ella observed flatly.

"Looks like it." Will sighed.

But Henry looked like he was about to erupt.

Chapter 47

HENRY'S FINGERS WERE like skittish horses at the starting gate of a race, just waiting to be unleashed. The gates opened and his thoughts galloped frantically out onto the screen in a jostling melée.

Hey. Truelove. You listen to me, you crazy witch. For someone who calls herself "Truelove," you have no heart whatsoever. Do you realize what you are putting my kids and me through? You are destroying our house. You are destroying us. My son was nearly ex-pelled. My daughter has an intense fear of germs and you now have her living in a house full of livestock. Strangers have literally invaded their bedrooms.

You think this is funny? Is that it? Well, let me tell you it is not. These gifts are doing thousands of dollars' worth of damage to our house that we cannot afford. I'll admit that neither the house nor our finances were in good shape before, but they are both a hell of a lot worse now.

I don't know how you're doing it, but IT HAS TO STOP. NOW. NOW!!!

When I find out who you are—and I WILL find out—I will make sure you are made to pay for what you've done. And I'm not just talking about the damage to our house. You will spend the rest of your days in jail. I will sue you for every penny you have... assuming you haven't spent every penny you have sending us all of these ridiculous, absurd "gifts."

Who are you? Make yourself known, you coward!

You're clearly someone near to us. You've infiltrated our internet. And you must have hypnotized me or something so that when I tried to tell the police about you, I spoke in an incoherent African language. Zulu. Judging by the inflection, I'm almost positive it was Zulu. And, yes, I know it was hypnosis. You see. I'm onto you.

You mess with me . . . I come after you.

You mess with my kids . . . I come after you with a vengeance.

You have been warned.

Henry pressed SEND and felt better. For a moment. But deep down, he knew there was nothing he could do. He couldn't tell the police. He had tried and failed. Maybe he could go to a lawyer. But, even if he didn't start spouting Zulu, what could he tell a lawyer that could be used to stop this woman? You can't issue a restraining order on someone whose name you don't know and whose address you don't have.

Besides, Ms. Truelove had hacked their internet and hypnotized him without him knowing. She was a criminal mastermind.

Strong words were his last and only weapon. Henry knew he was powerless. His only hope was that there were only two days left of the twelve in the Christmas carol, and, at the very least, that would end the arrival of gifts. Then the Sullivans could turn their minds to the disposal of the gifts.

Chapter 48

FROM THIS POINT onward, the gifts and the days blended together like eggnog and brandy. And the effects were just as nauseating. In retrospect, the overwhelmed Sullivans couldn't have told you what came in what order. Just that it all happened and they simply dealt with everything as best they could.

Considering their individual predicaments, it's surprising that they managed at all. Henry faced imminent unemployment along with the humiliation and ruin that would accompany it. Will was going to be beaten to within an inch of his life in front of the entire school. And Ella was never going to be allowed to paint another backdrop for another musical if she couldn't finish the current one before opening night tomorrow. Of course, that would only be an issue if she didn't fall into a disease-induced coma from the innumerable alien bugs and germs with which her house was currently crawling.

All of those issues would be enough to occupy any one family. But the Sullivans had the additional stress of "gifts" that kept arriving. It's a wonder that the entire family didn't go live in a tent under a highway somewhere... just for the peace and quiet.

After the arrival of the lords that morning, Henry took Will in the car to pick up hay and straw for the cows, leaving Ella in charge of the mayhem in the house. She attempted to clean, but it was like trying to sweep up dust in the Sahara. With the arrival of the lords, there were now scone crumbs all over everything, and not a piece of upholstery—including the curtains—had escaped the staining spill of tea. Leaping while holding a full teacup is a messy affair. In terms of damage, the lords ranked between the French hens, who sharpened their claws on every piece of furniture, and the geese, who were just wantonly destructive for no reason other than that they seemed to enjoy it.

And since the ancient washing machine had broken under the burden of all the dirty clothes, the houseguests had turned to hand-washing their things. So now fishnet stockings and dirndl aprons hung up drying around the house along with the lords' wool socks and various unmentionables.

Having whipped up a lunch of scrambled eggs for everyone, Ella tried communicating again with the lords. Wanting to get to the bottom of this whole situation, she enunciated carefully, "Who is Ms. Truelove?"

"I think the poor bairn must be hungry," declared Lord Gloatingham.

Ella rubbed her eyes. "No, not hungry. Annoyed. Just want to know who...is...Ms. Truelove? *Where*...is...she?"

"Someone offer her a sweetie," suggested Lord Twitch-Gelding.

"I don't want a damned sweetie! I want to know who Ms. Truelove is."

"Oh, I understand!" declared Lord Fitz-Crumpet triumphantly.

"Yes!" Ella shouted in a relieved manner. "*Thank* you. Finally."

"No. Sorry, my mistake." He shook his head. "Try the sweetie again."

Ella's irritated scream was interrupted, however, when a milkmaid came running in and tugged insistently on her arm. Ella followed her out to the garden, where one of the cows was lying down clearly in some discomfort.

"*Schwanger!*" several milkmaids shouted.

"What?" Ella responded.

"*Schwanger! Schwanger!*" They kept repeating.

"*Enceinte!*" a French dancer joined in unhelpfully.

But Ella had no idea what they were trying to tell her until Lord Twitch-Gelding, who was watching nonchalantly, said to Lord FitzCrumpet, "Looks like Daisy here is in *the maternal way.*"

"What?" said Ella turning to the lord. "Did you say this cow is pregnant?"

"Sorry," Lord FitzCrumpet enunciated loudly, "no-speak-o foreign-o."

"Poor Daisy is in some distress, though,"

said Lord Plummingford solemnly. "Dire complications."

"Looks like she's holding a one-way ticket," agreed Lord Lackchin. "Destination: pearly gates. To meet her bovine maker."

"She might *die*?" Ella shrieked. "Then do something! Help!"

But the lords simply walked away, suggesting brewing up a drop of the old Lapsang souchong for a pleasant change from Earl Grey.

The dancers and milkmaids were no more useful than the lords. They all just looked at Ella as if she were, for some reason, the only one who could act. So Ella did what she had to do . . . and called Mariana.

"Get the cow into the garage," instructed Mariana over the phone, "and make her comfortable. You'll be fine. I'll be on the phone with you the whole time."

But Ella wasn't fine. No sooner had they coaxed the cow into the garage when the old girl started to give birth. In a high-pitched, excitable voice, Ella described everything that was going on in front of an audience of tense, frightened lords, dancers, and milkmaids. It was taking too long for the calf to come out. Far too long. Finally, Mariana told Ella that the mother was too weak to push.

"There's no option. You're going to have to pull the calf out."

"WHAT?!" exclaimed Ella.

"Grab hold of its hooves and pull."

"Absolutely not!" She turned to the others. "You…or *you*…grab the hooves and pull!"

But nobody did.

"Oh, my *God*!" Ella shouted. And then, putting the phone on the ground, she pushed up her sleeves. With no time to retrieve oven mitts or rubber gloves or ski gloves, gardening gloves, driving gloves, opera gloves, goal-keeping gloves, bee-keeping gloves or any kind of glove whatsoever that might have offered *some* kind of protection, Ella was forced to grab hold of the emerging calf's slimy shins with her bare hands and began pulling with all her might. She pulled and pulled, encouraged by Mariana and cheered on by the dancers, milkmaids, and lords. Breaking into a sweat, Ella heaved until, with one last effort, the calf slid fully out from her mother and onto the garage floor.

Ella lay there exhausted in a puddle of whatever fluids accompany birth. But rather than being disgusted or scared of the potential bacteria that lurk inside of a cow, Ella stroked the calf's head lovingly and patted the mother's backside. And letting out a relieved, emotional laugh, she wiped her sweaty brow with a small part of the back of her wrist that was not covered in birth slime.

Chapter 49

LATER THAT AFTERNOON, Mariana arrived to check on the health of the Sullivans' newest four-legged houseguest. Having hurriedly corralled the dancers and lords into the house with instructions to stay quiet, the Sullivans kept Mariana confined to the garage. After a thorough examination under the protective eye of Ella, Mariana declared both mother and calf perfectly healthy.

"I'll just go inside and clean up," she said, holding up her filthy hands.

"There's a hose in the garden," suggested Henry a little too quickly.

"I might need to use a bathroom, too, actually," explained Mariana.

"It's broken," said Will hastily. "They all

are. Plumbing issues. Being sorted out right now."

At that moment, loud cancan music began blaring from the house.

"The plumbers," explained Ella. "They love their cabaret."

Joining the music was the sound of popping.

"That sounds like champagne corks…" Mariana ventured.

"No," replied Henry dismissively, only to be greeted with shouts from inside of "Champers!…Who wants bubbly?!… Shampoo, anyone?!"

"The plumbers must've found the problem. Celebration!" Will smiled.

"Ooooo-*kay*," sang Mariana dubiously. "I'll be going. I can take a hint."

"It's not that." Henry panicked a little. "I like having you here. I mean, we do. Just…the timing isn't great."

With that, an almighty crashing sound came from the house.

Henry winced. "I better check on the…plumbers," he said, leaving.

"Is everything okay?" Mariana asked Ella

and Will, who nodded as quickly and innocently as possible. Mariana leaned down to them and whispered with a smile, "Blink twice if you're being held captive."

Will and Ella smiled back, sorry they couldn't ask her to stay longer.

Chapter 50

THE COMPANY OF Mariana wasn't the only thing that the Sullivans lamented the loss of. There were a lot of things they missed. They missed peace, quiet, relaxation, cleanliness, their clothes, their rooms, and their sanity.

The party that started with champagne when Mariana was still there only grew. It grew louder, wilder, and more inconvenient for the Sullivans. German drinking songs were followed by French cabaret, which was followed by the Charleston and the foxtrot, which the lords taught the milkmaids and chorus girls.

Every time Henry poured himself a drink, a lord swooped in out of nowhere and relieved him of the full glass with a "Cheers, old boy" or "Just what the doctor ordered" or "It's like you read my mind, old bean."

Henry was shunted from room after room, including his own bedroom, where the geese had occupied his bed and refused to budge. To be fair, the duvet was goose down, so maybe it felt to them like a family reunion of sorts.

Finally, Henry went to the top of the house and quietly pulled down the ladder that led up to the attic. It was the one place that the houseguests had not yet colonized. There, he hoped he would find refuge from the hubbub.

Crouched down in the darkness lit only by the moon through a high round window, Henry pulled up the ladder after himself, closing the trapdoor and muffling the sounds of the party raging below.

"Hello," said a voice.

"Ow!" said a surprised Henry, having banged his head on a low beam. Rubbing the injured spot, he turned to see Will and Ella. They laughed at their predicament as fugitives in their own attic. All three had individually surmised that the attic was the last safe port in the tempest that was their house.

"How long do you think we'll have to live up here?" Will asked.

"No more than a year or so I'd imagine," Ella joked.

Henry was heartened to hear his son and daughter joking together again. He couldn't remember the last time he'd heard the two of them being nice to each other and enjoying each other's company. Despite that, he was concerned. He didn't want his kids to know, but when the clouds parted and the moon shone in, both children could see the worry on their father's face.

"Don't look so down," Will said. "They have to leave eventually."

Henry let out a small laugh. "It's not that. It's..." He let out a defeated sigh. "There's no way we can have Fringe and Grumpf here for dinner. Mariana was here for ten minutes, stayed in the garage the whole time, and still knew something was going on in the house. It's impossible. I'll have to call Fringe in the morning and let him know it's over."

"But if you do—" Ella started.

Henry cut her off. "Grumpf has hated me for years. If he didn't fire me this semester, he'd find a reason next semester or the one after. We'd only be delaying the inevitable. It'll be a new year in a week. Maybe it's time for a new *start*. There's a very fairly decent school in Maine that's looking for a history professor…"

"Maine?!" said Will, wishing he hadn't sounded quite so alarmed.

"What's wrong with Maine? It's very beautiful," suggested Henry.

"No. Nothing. Maine is…great," said Will with a forced smile.

"What's keeping us here?" said Henry, trying to whip up some enthusiasm. "Habit and laziness. For the price of this crumbling stack of bricks, we could get a new, modern, *renovated* place in Maine with all the mod cons. And, Ella, all the great artists moved to nature to hone their painting skills."

"Yeah, sure, that would be great," replied Ella, doing her very best to sound positive.

Had clouds not obscured the moon again,

the children would have seen a sincere and appreciative smile on Henry's face. "Fringe will give me an excellent reference. Now, let's get some sleep."

While gathering old ski clothes, crib mattresses, and anything soft to create beds for themselves, Ella picked up a blanket that unfurled along the floor until it released something from its folds: an antique music box. It had a brown wooden base on top of which stood an elegant painted ballerina. Ella looked at it, touching the face of the ballerina, feeling the cold porcelain on her fingertips. The raucous shouts and cancan music coming from the house beneath them faded as a hazy memory stirred in Ella. A memory of her mother holding her hands and dancing in a circle with her.

"Dad," she said, holding up the ballerina music box. "Wasn't this Mom's?"

Henry and Will came over to look.

Henry smiled. "Yes, it was hers. From when *she* was a little girl."

"I think she used to wind this up when she put us to bed, didn't she?" asked Will, trying to remember. "She'd let it play, saying we'd be asleep before the song ended. She was pretty much always right."

After a moment, Ella asked, "How did the tune go?"

"Was it...*da-da-duuum, da-da-duuum*..." sang Will tentatively.

"No. More like *dum-di-di-da, dum-di-di-da*..." said Ella, taking over.

Will disagreed, trying again, before Henry chimed in with his own version of how the tune surely went. After several confused minutes of battling variations, Will simply suggested they wind it up and end the debate once and for all.

But when they looked for the key, it was nowhere to be found. It wasn't taped to the bottom of the box or tied to the ballerina or tucked in anywhere that allowed tucking. They searched the blanket and the floor around them but couldn't find the key anywhere. It was gone. Lost. Separated from its box. And with it, any hope they had of making the comforting musical connection with their mother that they craved.

Reluctantly abandoning the search, they each curled up in their makeshift nest and individually tried to remember the tune. Although none of them succeeded, they each enjoyed the unexpected parade of long-forgotten memories that came instead. Especially Ella, who had the fewest of them. She, even more than the others, relished this newly unlocked treasure chest of tiny yet exquisite moments she had forgotten until now: licking batter-covered spoons in the kitchen. Shadow puppet shows on the living room wall. Planting seeds together in the vegetable beds. The soothing tickle of nails on her back as she drifted off to sleep.

On the Eleventh Day

Chapter 51

THE NEXT MORNING, Will and Henry walked downstairs to witness something approaching a miracle. The entire house was a veritable hive of positive activity. Lord Buffton was mopping the floors. Lord Twitch-Gelding was vacuuming the carpets. And Lord Fitz-Crumpet was carrying a toilet scrubber over his shoulder like a Coldstream Guard into the downstairs bathroom, where he began scrubbing with vigor. In fact, all ten aristocrats were cleaning like the revolution had happened and they were desperate to blend in with the masses.

The scene in the kitchen was even more miraculous. The milkmaids were stationed around the room. Two were double boiling multiple pots of milk to pasteurize it. They then passed the clean milk to other milkmaids who were churning it into cream, adding salt to pat it into butter, or stirring in cultures and rennet to produce great balls of delicious cheese.

Meanwhile, the French dancing ladies had taken over the dining room, where large sacks of flour and sugar were stacked up in order to make tray after tray of flaky croissants, baguettes, and other delectable pastries, the base ingredients of which were goose eggs, freshly pasteurized milk, and homemade butter.

Waving the fog of flour out of the air, Will and Henry made their way through the dining room to the kitchen, where they found Ella, like a conductor in the middle of an orchestra of domestic help.

"What's going on?" marveled Henry.

"We're getting ready for the dinner party tonight," stated Ella, who was effortlessly whipping up a tornado of eggs to make cheese and herb omelets for whoever was hungry. "I thought about it, Dad, and, uh...I don't want to move to Maine. I don't want to leave this house. And I don't want you to lose your job."

As Henry struggled for a response, Will added sheepishly, "I don't really want those things, either."

"So we're going to have the provost and the dean here tonight," stated Ella, "and we're going to have an excellent dinner, starting with cheese and herb soufflé. Main course of fish, which you'll have to go out and buy. Nothing expensive, just some trout maybe. I'm off meat anyway since Leggy was born."

"Leggy?" questioned Henry, interrupting Ella's flow.

"The calf. That's what I named her. Get it? Leggy? Calf? Anyway, can you believe it, the lords found vegetables still growing in the garden. Carrots, onions, tomatoes. It's incredible. And the dancers are making dessert. You know the French are the best in the world at pastries and cakes."

"But...how did you get them to do all this?" Henry asked, watching a milkmaid put another glistening yellow brick on a wall of butter she seemed to be constructing.

"Gestures, pointing, that kind of thing. I'm not much of a talker anyway," Ella rambled on.

"You are this morning. Are you okay?" Will asked gently. "I mean, you're kind of hyped up."

"Me? No. Don't think so. Just normal. I mean, I did get up early to do the research online and flick through Mom's recipes, of course..." Ella paused to take a sip from a mug.

Sniffing the mug, Henry asked, "Is that...coffee?"

"Hm? This? Yeah. Thought I'd have a little cup o' joe, right? I mean, what's the harm...*heyyyy!*" Ella shouted as Henry plucked the mug from her hands.

"I think you've probably had enough coffee for a twelve-year-old."

"It's great that you got the lords cleaning up and you're taking care of dinner," said Will, "but, Ella, what about all the birds. And cows? They're all over the house. There's no way we can control all of them for the whole time Grumpf and Fringe are here."

"*We* can't. But Mariana can," said Ella with a wink, which was something neither Henry nor Will had ever seen her do before.

At that moment, the doorbell rang and Ella volunteered to answer it. Will and Henry pulled her back and urgently explained that if Mariana saw all the people here, she'd want to know where they all came from. And they couldn't tell her that some mysterious internet stranger had been somehow delivering them to the house. She'd run away screaming.

"Don't worry. It's taken care of. Watch," said Ella as she opened the door, revealing Mariana standing there wrapped up against the cold.

Mariana wiped her feet on the mat and came in, handing her coat to Henry and rubbing some warmth back into her nose, which had gone a rather festive faintly red color. She then stopped totally still as she, for the first time, was confronted by the crowds of people, the activity, and the mess. Several days ago, when she'd last been inside the house, it was a bit overrun. Now it was like the international terminal at JFK airport. Only messier. The level of destruction and deterioration was cataclysmic.

Henry noted the dumbstruck look on Mariana's face but tried to move past it.

"Mariana, how nice of you to come. How are you?" he asked nervously, hyperconscious of Lord FitzCrumpet behind him leaping in the air while waving a feather duster to clean cobwebs off the top of the bookshelves.

"I'm fine, thank you. How are—"

"Uh-uh-uh-uh," tutted Ella authoritatively, "*that* is a question I believe."

"Right," conceded Mariana. "When we spoke on the phone, I promised no questions…although I have to admit when I promised that, I did not think I'd have quite as many questions as I do." She craned her neck to see the nine stocking-clad can-can dancers up to their elbows in flour and dough in the dining room and the milk-maids running the dairy-product factory in the kitchen.

"But a promise is a promise, right?" Ella pointed out.

Mariana nodded. "Absolutely. No questions.

Someday, however, I'll expect a full explanation."

"Thank you," said Henry. "We need all the help we can get."

Among all the hustle and bustle, Henry made Mariana a hot coffee with fresh milk and handed her possibly the flakiest, freshest, French-est croissant on the eastern seaboard. He then proceeded to tell her about tonight's dinner and its importance to them as a family. That much he *could* explain in detail. She listened attentively, gleaning that they wanted her to use her animal-taming skills to keep all livestock hidden away from the guests for the duration of the meal.

"Any questions?" asked Henry.

"Dozens," replied Mariana with a smile. "Literally dozens. But I know they'll have to wait for another day."

Chapter 52

IT WAS A busy afternoon for all of them as there was much to do before the arrival of their dinner guests. Ella—after a well-deserved nap—had to rush to school to finish the sets before tomorrow's opening night. The painted backdrops were not what Ella had imagined when she volunteered to design them but were the best she could do within the constraints dictated by Sally Kensington and the immutable laws of time. Maybe she would have done better had there been fewer cows and dancing ladies in her house, but that's surely true of all of us.

"I preferred the previous sets, Ella," said a singsongy voice.

Shocked that someone was talking to her—

and knew her name—Ella looked up to see leading man and Swedish demigod Gus Gustavson smiling down at her. Looking into his green eyes, she melted a little but found herself almost involuntarily asking out of nowhere, "Why do you need to beat up the boy who stole your bike?"

Although surprised by the directness of the question, Gus answered in a matter-of-fact manner. "Because he stole my bike."

"Maybe he's sorry," Ella ventured boldly. "Maybe he had a reason for stealing your bike."

"I'm sure both of those things are true. But actions have consequences. Imagine if we let all criminals go unpunished for their crimes. Avarice would run rampant. The weak would be trampled. Do you *want* the weak to be trampled?"

"No. I don't want *anyone* to be trampled," admitted Ella.

"So you agree I have to punish him if you love liberty and order! *Do* you love liberty and order?"

What else could Ella do except agree, saying,

"I do love liberty. And order happens to be one of my favorite states of being."

"You're funny," said Gus, smiling, before walking away.

Nobody had ever called her funny before. Unless they meant *funny* as in *odd, bizarre,* or *awkward.* But Gus seemed to mean it in a positive way. He certainly smiled when he said it. A nice warm smile. A smile like a hammock you want to lie in and read a book while sipping a drink and enjoying the sunset.

"I think he likes you," said Suzanne, shaking Ella from her nonalcoholic piña colada dreams.

Ella let out an awkward combination laugh-snort that she was glad Gus was not close enough to hear. But then it dawned on her with horror and a gnawing sense of disappointment. "I was trying to help Will, but I think I just threw my brother under the bus."

"Oh, for sure," agreed Suzanne, who'd witnessed the whole exchange. "Will has your handprints on his back and tire marks on his face, no question about it."

It turns out, however, Ella need not have been so worried.

When she arrived home, she saw that Will had taken his fate into his own hands. And then placed it in the soft, pink, manicured grasp of the ten lords, who as English aristocrats were, of course, fully schooled in several forms of chivalric combat.

They had spent the morning instructing Will in the art of fencing. With an umbrella. It turns out Will was a natural and could parry, thrust, advance, retreat, and lunge with lightning speed and deadly accuracy. And when Will's proficiency in fencing was established, they had then all stripped to the waist—not a pretty sight for the most part—and taught Will the basics of boxing, Marquis of Queensbury rules, of course, which Will soon mastered with devastating effect as evidenced by Lord Twitch-Gelding sitting at the side of the room with a bloody tissue in each nostril.

"Wait, that's not it, Ella. Watch this..." Will said, pulling a yo-yo from his pocket, flinging it straight out and accurately knocking the hat off the head of a terrified Lord Gloatingham before zipping it back in.

"Wow!" said Ella, impressed. "The lords taught you to do that, too?"

"No, you ding-dong." Will laughed. "The pipers taught me that."

"The...*pipers*?"

Will directed Ella's gaze out the window to see eleven poncho-clad South American men, with floppy felt hats obscuring their faces, blowing tunefully on panpipes to the apparent delight of the geese. Will explained that they arrived shortly after Ella left that morning.

"Hey," Ella exclaimed brightly, "if they speak Spanish, that means Mariana can talk to them!"

"No dice. Wrong dialect." Will sighed. "And the lords, somehow, still can't understand us either," he said, turning to Lord Lackchin. "Can you, you inbred old fop?"

"Yes, yes, nearly teatime. I'm parched," replied the lord obligingly.

Chapter 53

WHILE ELLA WENT to the kitchen to oversee the final preparations of dinner, Mariana was upstairs dividing the birds between bedrooms, bathrooms, and closets. She was filling a bowl with Perrier water for the French hens when she heard Henry swearing angrily in the next room. She poked her head in to find Henry hunched over with his back to her.

"Move! Move, you damn thing!" Henry swore. "Come *ON!*"

"Hello?" Mariana interrupted.

Henry whipped around, looking surprised and somewhat embarrassed.

"Is there a problem?" Mariana asked before correcting herself. "Sorry, that was a question. I mean...you seem to have a problem." Then noticing that his hands were covering the crotch area of his pants, she quickly added, "Maybe I should come back later."

Henry stopped her from leaving, explaining that he was putting on his pants and caught his shirttail. He removed his hands, revealing several inches of shirt protruding from the zipper. "And now the damn thing won't open. It's stuck fast. I can't zip them up. I can't take them off."

As if to prove the point he heaved at the zipper unsuccessfully until he was slightly red in the face before slapping his hands onto his sides as a sign of defeat and frustration. "I'm stuck! I'll have to, I don't know, wrap a sweater around my waist. Or wear a long coat? Maybe I can say I have a chill."

Despite the gravity of the situation, Mariana couldn't help but let a small laugh escape. She saw the thunder on Henry's face and held up an apologetic hand. "I'm sorry. I'm sorry. It's just...you just can't catch a break!"

Henry's annoyance at her callousness only lasted a moment before it gave way and he found himself joining in with a laugh of his own. And with that laugh, a lot of his tension was disbursed.

The two of them giggled for a while before Mariana told him to wait there. She disappeared into the bathroom, returning with a bar of soap.

"Just rub this on the zipper. It'll act as a lubricant."

"Really?"

"It should work. I'd do it for you, but…"

"Uh, no, that's okay," said Henry, taking the soap and running it over the stuck zipper. Then with a mighty heave, the shirt and zipper gave way and Henry was a free man once again. Zipping himself up correctly this time, Henry asked how it was all going with the birds.

Mariana explained it was a simple matter of supplying each species with the diversion they respond to. For example, French hens, naturally enough, find the songs of Edith Piaf comforting. Geese, who have a broader sense of humor, like the slapstick antics of old Charlie Chaplin movies. Calling birds are mesmerized by *Animal Planet*, while, predictably, only Tchaikovsky can keep swans subdued. And the cows all seemed perfectly happy in the garage listening to early Britney Spears.

"Britney Spears? *Really?*" Henry said, his face scrunched up, as he struggled to get the length right on his tie.

"Don't judge them," Mariana said, taking control of the tie and adjusting it perfectly. "There." She took a step back to look at him.

"Would you hire this man to educate the next generation of overqualified, unemployed intellectuals?" Henry asked.

"Absolutely," she responded, before tugging his beard and adding, "assuming the class you're teaching is Modern Caveman 101?" She laughed and left the room.

Henry turned to glance at himself in the mirror. He ran a hand over his unkempt beard, the result of laziness and neglect rather than adherence to any hipster trend.

Ten minutes later, with both his beard *and* hair neatly combed and trimmed, Henry looked like a new man and was ready to go downstairs. The dean and the provost would be arriving any moment and Henry knew exactly what he needed before their arrival.

A stiff drink.

As recently as two days ago, that would've been an easy task. There were any number of alcoholic beverages to choose from around the house. Now, however, it was an impossibility. The previous night's party apparently had been more liquid than he thought, and, with time ticking away, Henry scrambled through cabinets fruitlessly looking for a not-empty bottle until, in a forgotten drawer in an obscure cabinet, he found something hidden there long ago.

Not a bottle, though. A book. *His* book. The historical book that, had he finished it, might have made him dean instead of Grumpf. His wife, Katie, must have been proofreading it for him before she died and put the pages in that cabinet. This is where it had been for five years.

He flicked through the yellowing manu-script, admiring the bold red lines she'd drawn through the dull bits and the smiley faces she'd drawn by the clever bits. He was heartened to see there were a lot more smiley faces, tick marks, and occasionally double tick marks (for the bits she really enjoyed) than crossed-out paragraphs.

A knock at the door pulled Henry back to reality. A reality he would dauntingly have to face without a drink. The thought of it sent a shiver of panic up his spine. If this night went badly, not only would he lose his job, he'd lose any chance of a glowing recommendation from Dr. Fringe to help secure a new job.

Chapter 54

"COME IN, COME IN," Henry warmly greeted his guests with a show of enthusiasm worthy, at the very least, of a Golden Globe if not an Oscar.

After the taking of coats and general introductions, Dean Grumpf and Provost Fringe followed Will, Ella, Henry, and Mariana into the living room, where the loose-jawed guests were struck dumb by the state of the place. While it was considerably cleaner than it had been in ten days, to outsiders the room—and the house as a whole—still looked like the First Battle of Bull Run had taken place in it.

Fringe, who knew that things were tough at home for his friend, noted that they were far worse than he ever imagined. Not knowing that there had been pecking, scratching, clawing wildlife in the living room, the only reasonable explanation Dr. Fringe could conjure was that Henry's children must have been gnawing on the furniture.

Dean Grumpf brushed some dirt off a cushion and dropped onto—and *through*—the sofa, the springs and stuffing having been entirely eaten away by the geese. Henry and Mariana rushed forward to pull out the dean, who looked like he was being eaten by a voracious couch.

Henry apologized, offering the dean a wonky chair. Grumpf did his best to get comfortable, adjusting the black patch he was still wearing over his pecked eyeball.

"Drinks!" Henry offered brightly before remembering the house was devoid of any alcoholic beverages that might help lubricate the evening.

"Yes, thank you," said Fringe. "What do you have?"

"Uhhhhhh…" Henry stalled. "There's the… tap water, uh, and… and there's… uh, fresh… milk," he said brightly, trying to really sell the guests on the idea of a tall glass of cold milk.

Seeing her father flounder, Ella intervened. "How about tea? I'll go get it."

She left the room, running upstairs, bursting into Will's bedroom, where she found the geese watching *The Three Stooges* while the lords polished their shotguns.

"Tea! I need tea!" Ella whisper-shouted at them, miming the act of pouring tea from a teapot.

"Charades!" Lord Lackchin clapped softly. "I love charades!"

"Phone call!" guessed Lord Gloatingham.

"*Teaaaaaaaa,*" Ella tried again, wildly miming sipping from a cup.

"Chapstick?" concluded Lord FitzCrumpet.

At that point, Ella saw Lord Twitch-Gelding pouring tea for Lord Lackchin. She simply swiped the pot away from them and fled the room, slamming the door unfortunately on a goose who understandably let out an ear-splitting "WAAAAAAAAAK!!!"

Whispering profuse apologies to the injured goose, she pushed it back into the room and made haste downstairs, where a concerned Fringe and Grumpf asked what that noise was.

"Noise?" she responded innocently. "What noise? I didn't hear a WAAAAAAAAK noise. Tea? WAAAAAAAAK!"

Staring at the shrieking child, Fringe and Grumpf did not pry any further. They were barely two sips into their tea when Henry, trying and failing to sound casual, urged everyone to move into the dining room for dinner. He didn't want this evening to last any longer than it had to. And to be honest, Fringe and Grumpf were inclined to agree.

Against all odds, however, dinner seemed to go well. The egg and cheese–based dish that Ella cooked using her mother's old recipe were excellent. And, more importantly, the gifts largely remained quiet. There was the occasional thud or thump, but the Sullivans explained them away as the idiosyncratic creaks made by an old Victorian house.

The saving grace, however, was that Dean Grumpf never tired of the sound of his own voice. He was a never-ending fountain of ignorance, opinions, contradictions, and justifications, interrupted only by Ella periodically screaming "WAAAAAAAAK," since she felt the need to keep up the pretense. But even that didn't disturb the flow from Grumpf, who was a bore of Olympian proportions and managed to cause offense with almost every utterance.

There was a minor scare for the Sullivans when they realized they had neglected to lock away the turtle doves, who were, as always, perched high above Grumpf's and Fringe's gaze on a light fixture, from where two small pellets dropped from the backside of one—or both—of the turtle doves and landed in Grumpf's cheese soufflé with a gentle *plip-plop*. Each family member thought about saying something, but decided against it.

Grumpf was, in fact, complimenting the earthiness of the soufflé when he was interrupted by a surprised Dr. Fringe.

"Oh, my goodness!" Fringe said.

They followed his gaze to the doorway, where Leggy the calf had wandered coolly into the dining room. The Sullivans had no idea how she escaped from the garage, but here she was in all her bovine glory, swishing her tail and licking her nose.

Henry broke into a sweat, trying to think up an explanation.

"Is that a..." began Grumpf.

"Rover!" shouted Mariana. "Bad dog! I thought I left you tied up outside with a nice juicy bone. Bad dog!"

"Dog?" said Grumpf. "But that's not a—"

"Dog?" Mariana interrupted. "No. You're right. How very perceptive. Rover is, of course...a *hound*. A Guatemalan cow hound."

"Cow hound?! But that's a—" Grumpf continued incredulously.

"Yes," Mariana preempted again, "a very rare breed of dog. Nobody outside of Guatemala has even heard of them. Is there no end to your knowledge? You are quite brilliant."

"Well." Grumpf nodded modestly. "I do...read a lot."

The flattery seemed to work on Grumpf. And, as for Fringe, if Grumpf was willing to accept it, who was he to object?

Mariana and Will were already pulling the

calf out of the room before any more questions could be asked...or cloven hooves could be studied. Ella screamed "WAAAAAAAAAK" again to distract them and asked Dean Grumpf about his book, which seemed to do the trick.

As long as Grumpf could hear the sound of his own voice, he seemed happy. And that was the goal of the dinner: for Grumpf to be happy and therefore inclined to retain Henry in his current job. A secretive thumbs-up from Fringe to Henry seemed to indicate things were going well.

Chapter 55

CLEARING PLATES FROM the table brought all three Sullivans into the kitchen at the same time. There, they quietly high-fived one another, collapsed into chairs, and laughed at Grumpf's ridiculousness.

They had made it through to dessert. They were a slice of tart away from the finishing line. If they all ate quickly and feigned great fatigue, it could all be over within twenty glorious minutes. Then, with Grumpf and Fringe out of the house, they could open all doors and return to the familiar, unfettered mayhem that ruled the abode these days without the added fear of discovery. That moment would offer the relief of letting out your belt after a particularly filling meal.

The brief respite in the kitchen also gave the three of them the opportunity to share a moment of Mariana appreciation. She had been a marvel. There was no way they'd have been able to host this evening without her.

"I mean," said Will, "Guatemalan *cow hound*? She's an evil genius."

"All credit to you, Will," said Ella. "After all, you called her the day the cows arrived. Without that, she might have left our lives altogether."

Will looked at her, puzzled. "Me? I didn't call her that day." He shrugged. "When she turned up, I assumed Dad had called her."

"No. I didn't," said Henry, his forehead furrowed. "I didn't even know she'd stopped over until I got home and Ella told me."

"Are you sure *you* didn't call her, Ella?" Will probed.

"Of course I'm sure," she retorted. "Why would I have called her? I didn't even know cows had turned up. I'd left for school before they arrived."

"But," puzzled Will, "if none of us called

her, how would she have known that we needed her?"

"She wouldn't," said Ella.

"Unless..." Henry began, but then stopped.

An unwelcome thought was formulating in his mind and creeping into his consciousness. Something diabolical and scary. A thought he tried to wish away, but it was like trying to wish away dark clouds on a winter day. And the same thought was occurring to Ella and Will. No one dared express it out loud. Except Will...

"Unless *she* sent them to us," he whispered forebodingly.

"No!" Ella whispered. "That's impossible... isn't it?"

The Sullivans stared at one another in semi-disbelief.

"Let's just think about this," said Will. "She turned up on day three. Out of the blue. All the neighbors deny calling Animal Protection Services. And, Dad, did you ever actually check her credentials?"

Henry admitted it hadn't even occurred to him. In fact, she could have been anyone in a tan uniform with an animal badge on it. If truth be told, none of them had even heard of Animal Protection Services until she said she worked for them.

"She certainly knows a lot about all the birds and animals that have arrived," Will continued. "She identified them all immediately. And now that I think about it, she's been surprisingly unsurprised by everything. You saw the look on Grumpf and Provost Fringe's faces when the cow walked in. Mariana never looked like that."

Ella's eyes watered slightly. "She can't be Ms. Truelove."

"If not Mariana, who?" asked Will.

Nobody had an answer. It was a question they had all been grappling with for almost two weeks. And none of them had come up with anything even approaching a reasonable answer. Mariana knew where they lived so could have hacked their internet if that was indeed how Ms. Truelove communicated with them. And if, as Henry thought, he had been put under some kind of hypnosis that prevented him from telling anyone about the gifts, Mariana was one of very few people who had had ample opportunity to do so to him.

What had been a moment of celebration had in a matter of minutes turned very dark.

"Hey!" said a cheery voice from the doorway.

They looked around to see Mariana entering the kitchen. Sitting down with them, she whispered, "Real nice of you to leave me out there on my own with them."

When they didn't respond, she noticed the concerned looks on their faces. "What? I thought it was going well. Why do you all look like a camel licked your ice-cream cone? That happened to me once. It's disgusting." She laughed.

They didn't.

"Seriously. What's up?"

"Mariana...did you do this to us?" asked Henry.

"Do what?" asked Mariana.

"*This,*" said Will. "The birds. The animals. The *gifts.*"

"Ella," Mariana appealed for an explanation, "what is he talking about?"

"Oh, Mariana," cried Ella, tears rolling

down her cheeks, "why would you do this? Why did it have to be you?"

While a confused and hurt Mariana listened to the accusations in the kitchen, in the dining room the conversation had ground to a halt.

"I wonder what they're doing in there?" asked Fringe, desperate for someone to return so he didn't have to engage with Dean Grumpf on his own.

"I don't know," said Grumpf, who then lowered his voice. "I had no idea how bad it was at home for Professor Sullivan. This place is a pigsty. And then there's the little girl who keeps screaming. I heard the boy was recently expelled from school. And the girlfriend has the world's ugliest dog. I mean, *yerch*."

"You think that's his girlfriend?" asked Fringe.

"I assumed. Anyway, there's no way we can fire the man. It would be too cruel with all the other awful things going on in his life."

That was what Fringe needed to hear. His plan had worked. Not in the way he *thought* it would work. But the result was the same.

"Any idea where there's a bathroom in this dump? I think there was something in the soufflé that didn't entirely agree with me."

"There's one at the top of the stairs if I remember correctly." Dr. Fringe pointed upstairs, assuming Mariana must be in the one downstairs.

Without any of the Sullivans present to prevent him, Dean Grumpf rose from the table, walked into the hallway, and began the trek upstairs. With each labored step, he was inching closer and closer to discovering the secrets they were desperate to keep hidden. And all the people who could intercept him were entirely distracted in the kitchen, pushing Mariana to just admit her true identity. Absorbed in the interrogation, they didn't hear the plodding footsteps or floorboards creaking.

Left entirely to his own devices, Grumpf simply puffed his way to the top of the stairs and paused, confronted by a number of shut doors. Without giving it any thought—which is how Grumpf did most things—he reached for the closest door, twisted the handle, and opened it.

As luck would have it, he guessed correctly. It was the bathroom. But unfortunately for him, there were four calling birds dozing peacefully in the total darkness of the room. As the gleaming light of the hallway replaced the serene blackness, Grumpf was immediately enveloped by the terrifying noise of four calling birds screaming at the top of their lungs.

A thunderstruck, petrified Grumpf stumbled back, barging straight into Ella's room, where he found eight powerfully built German ladies changing into their nightclothes. The indignant milkmaids slapped this accidental Peeping Tom across the face, pushing the bewildered man from fraülein to fraülein, each taking their turn to forcefully strike him until he fell back out of the door and flat on his face on the hallway floor.

When he looked up, he caught sight of his old nemesis, Alan, the partridge chick, who was looking at Grumpf's last remaining good eye like it was a thermal exhaust port on the Death Star and he was Luke Skywalker.

Grumpf immediately scrambled to dive

through the closest door, which happened to be a linen closet. He slammed the door protectively after him but came out screaming a moment later when the three French hens—not happy about being disturbed right in the middle of their favorite song—violently and rapidly pecked his legs, drawing blood up and down his shins. He burst out of the closet just in time to be chased by a flock of peeved swans coming straight for him.

The best he could do was seek refuge behind the last remaining door. He burst into Will's room only to find himself immediately staring down the business end of a 20-bore sidelock-ejector over-and-under shotgun held by a pink-faced peer of the British realm who was himself surrounded by nine other gun-toting aristocrats and a number of geese, all ogling strangely at him.

"Steady on, old boy," said Lord Lackchin. "These things can be quite dangerous. Bloody lucky it's not loaded."

Dean Grumpf didn't stick around to find out, though. Terror-struck, he was already sprinting full tilt down the stairs when his ears rang with a loud bang and he felt the whoosh of buckshot pass within inches of his head on the way to peppering the wall above him.

"Sorry! My mistake," a British voice called from upstairs.

Screaming, Grumpf arrived at the bottom of the stairs, where he collided with a tearful Mariana exiting the kitchen at the exact same moment, her forehead connecting at speed with the soft bone of Grumpf's nose. There was an ominous cracking sound as the dean let out a high-pitched shriek of pain.

"My nose! My nose!" Grumpf moaned as blood gushed over his mouth, down his chin, and soaked his shirt.

The Sullivans, now convinced that they had been entirely wrong about her, had been following right behind Mariana. They were just in time to witness the full complement of birds, cows, dancers, milkmaids, lords, and pipers pouring out of their hiding places and crowding the ground floor of the house.

Mariana did not hang about. She pushed past everyone and was already at the front door.

Henry tried to reach her, calling for her to stop, but there were too many obstacles now blocking his way. Including Dr. Fringe, who did not look amused. The front door slammed loudly after Mariana.

Despite the mass of humans and animal species gathered, the house fell eerily quiet and still. Everyone, including the birds and cows, just stared at Henry, all seeming to understand the gravity of the situation. The only noise piercing the frosty silence was the occasional *plip* of the blood rolling off Grumpf's chin and hitting the wooden floorboards.

Grabbing a napkin and holding it over his nose to stanch the flow, Dean Grumpf was beginning to feel faint. But he had enough strength to raise his arm, point at Henry, and, with his voice trembling with anger, say, "Professor Sullivan... you... are... fired."

On the Twelfth Day

Chapter 56

THE NEXT DAY was Christmas Eve. In some countries, Christmas Eve is a bigger celebration than Christmas Day.

In Canada, Sweden, and Denmark, families open their presents on Christmas Eve. In Italy, they have the Feast of the Seven Fishes, during which they eat a lot of fish. Seven, I'd imagine. The French delight in making Buche de Noel, which is a sponge cake frosted and decorated to look exactly like a log. It's a mystery why a dessert masquerading as the limb of a tree would be delightful and appetizing, but they seem to like it. In Russia, on Christmas Eve, they make Kutya, a gloopy mixture of grains, nuts, seeds, and honey that is eaten from a communal bowl as a display of unity and a blatant disregard for hygiene. In China, Christmas Eve is the biggest shopping day of the year and they hand each other apples wrapped in cellophane.

In the Sullivan house, however, there was little to celebrate. They couldn't even celebrate their discovery of the true identity of Ms. Truelove, for it was clear that Mariana was indeed *not* Ms. Truelove. Her confused looks, tearful expression, and sincere, prolonged denials convinced them of that. She explained that she had been unaware that there were cows at the house when she decided to stop by. She'd simply come to check on them because she was in the neighborhood, liked the Sullivans, and wanted to help.

That hadn't occurred to them. The sad truth was, they weren't in the habit of experiencing kindness and it had been quite a long time since anyone had liked them. And nobody had wanted to help them in ages. It was a sad reflection of where they'd sunk to as a family in the five years since their mother had died.

Now, the one person who had cared was

gone. Chased away, insulted by the Sullivans themselves.

If the "gifts" had seemed to understand what was happening last night, this morning they did not let on. They went about their daily chaos as usual. The swans were a-swimming, the geese a-laying, and the ladies were dancing. Maids a-milked, lords a-leaped, and the pipers piped. When the drummers arrived—in the form of twelve silent, muscular Japanese monks—they beat soulfully on their taiko drums after being shown into the house by a resigned Will, who gently told them to make themselves at home.

The house no longer felt like home to Will, his sister, or their father. In fact, the Sullivans felt like squatters, listlessly tucked up in the attic all morning unable to face the scene of the previous night's utter defeat downstairs.

Finally, tired of feeling disconsolate and in need of just getting away from the noise and activity below, Henry roused his children, told them to put on their coats, and took them outside for an excursion. It was an unusual activity for the Sullivans, in that all three were participating willingly and it involved being nice to the neighbors.

They went house to house, lugging heavy baskets, knocking on doors, and handing their surprised neighbors gifts of homemade butter, great balls of cheese, parcels of herbs, and flaky French pastries. The neighbors eyed or sniffed the gifts suspiciously, but Henry assured them they were meant as an apology for his somewhat intolerant behavior toward them over the years as well as for the extremely inconvenient collection of noises and smells emanating from their house over the past twelve days.

If the neighbors were suspicious about the comestible gifts, they were doubly wary of Henry's apology. But his sincerity, buoyed by Will and Ella's exhausted yet honest faces, eventually won the day. The gifts and apologies were accepted with grace and appreciation, allowing the Sullivans to feel a little better about themselves and their situation.

Chapter 57

By 2 p.m. that day, a large crowd had gathered in the alley behind the school. Students were jostling for position, sitting atop huge garbage dumpsters or shimmied up lampposts. It was a sold-out event. In fact, Fash and Noodle had made over fifty dollars conning students to buy tickets from them.

There was barely an empty space. The school musical later that evening would be lucky to attract numbers like this. But the school musical didn't promise what this event did: the total destruction and humiliation of a student.

The crowds parted as Gus Gustavson arrived majestically on his bike, skidding to a halt in the middle of the circle of fans cheering for him. Any hopes of an unbiased crowd disappeared in an instant. As the cheers died down, the audience began checking the time on their phones and other devices. Maybe one or two old-fashioned types checked the time on a watch.

A rumor rippled through the throng that Will wasn't going to show up. That he'd absconded. That he was on a flight to Canada at this very moment to undergo plastic surgery and start a new life as a lumberjack named Pierre La Forrestiere. But those rumors dissipated when a dull, rhythmic drumming could be heard in the distance.

The sound came closer and closer until Will himself rounded the corner into the alleyway accompanied by the twelve taiko drummers who had arrived that morning. He held his head up high, displaying an almost noble bearing that impressed more than a few in the crowd, which parted to allow him and his entourage through.

Will arrived in the middle of the circle, face-to-face with Gus, who looked down at Will and smiled.

"I'm glad you showed up. I shall remember your courage while I beat you and I will take pity."

"Likewise," said Will, trying not to sound nervous.

Gus laughed. "I like you, Will. You are a worthy foe. Now...let's fight."

As Gus removed his jacket, revealing his rippling muscles stretching his tight T-shirt, Will held out his hand and a taiko drummer threw him an umbrella, which Will caught, adopting the fencing en garde pose.

A ripple of soft laughter rolled through the crowd.

"He thinks he's Zorro!" shouted a voice that Will recognized as Bean's.

"Tear him up, Gus!" rose the unmistakable nasal tones of Fash, who then added, "Nothing personal, Will, but I have five bucks on Gus breaking your arm. You understand."

Will understood perfectly. He understood the meaning of friendship and that he had been looking for it in the wrong place.

More voices urged Gus to do increasingly violent things to Will.

Only one voice shouted out, "You can d-d-d-do it, Will!!!" It was a weak, stammering voice, but the shock of someone actually rooting for Will created a hush as people wondered who it was.

It was, of course, Benny. The old friend Will had treated so badly. And, yet, here he was risking ridicule to offer a little encouragement to the unpopular underdog in this battle. The crowd erupted in laughter, pointing at Benny and shouting insults. But Benny firmly stared at Will as if imparting strength and belief through eye contact.

Benny is right. I can do this, thought Will, formulating the exact plan of attack: *A lightning-quick thrust-lunge-redoublement-recover-balestra-jump and flèche attack to finish him off.*

Will drew a deep breath and, hoping to catch Gus by surprise, ran shouting with the tip of the umbrella unwavering toward Gus's chest. Will was sure that the first blow would unnerve and unbalance Gus, while the subsequent barrage of blows would so disorient and injure his opponent that he would be obliged to beg for mercy.

That was the theory at least.

In reality, things were quite different. Gus simply grabbed the umbrella in midair, stopping all forward momentum dead, causing Will to release the umbrella and fall into a mucky puddle. A composed Gus broke the makeshift weapon over his knee and tossed it casually off to the side.

Most people would be disconsolate at this point. Not Will, however, because he had a Plan C. C? What happened to Plan B, I hear you ask. Surely after Plan A and before Plan C, there must be a Plan B. Well, Plan B was bare-knuckle boxing, and in the cool light of day, that was patently absurd. So Will skipped straight to Plan C. The yo-yo!

As he picked himself up out of the puddle, Will withdrew the yo-yo from his pocket and whipped it straight toward the forehead of Gus, like a modern-day David and Swedish Goliath. Unfortunately for Will, in his haste, he had failed to secure the string to his finger.

So when Gus rather casually leaned six inches to his left, allowing the yo-yo to fly harmlessly past his head, it simply carried on and hit a trash can before bouncing onto the ground. Admittedly it made a considerable dent in the trash can and might have made a similar dent in Gus...had it been on target...which it wasn't.

Now, having failed with Plan A and Plan C (and having discounted Plan B as discussed), Will was out of plans. Plan D could only be one thing: bleeding profusely from a number of wounds and limping painfully to the closest hospital.

Gus approached, his shadow casting Will into darkness. Literally and figuratively.

"I had hoped for a little more. Oh, well," said Gus, cracking his knuckles, drawing back his arm, and aiming his fist at Will's cheek.

Will held his breath and squeezed his eyes shut, awaiting the coming blow and the pain that would accompany it.

"Stop!" a voice rang out.

Everyone looked around to see who had the audacity to interrupt the pummeling that they had all come to see.

"Oh, hello, Ella," said Gus pleasantly. "Can this wait? I'm in the middle of something."

"No, it can't wait," she said, striding up to Gus. "Leave my brother alone."

Will was, for the first time in a long while, consumed by an older-sibling concern for the safety and reputation of his sister. "Ella," he whispered insistently. "What are you doing? Go! You do not want to get into this."

She ignored him. "Gus, I have a challenge for you. I win, you let Will go scot-free. You win, you get to beat the crap out of Will, *and* he polishes your bike every week for the entire coming year."

Gus was intrigued. It was true, he hated polishing his bike, but loved his bike to be nice and shiny. "What is the challenge?"

"You and me. Arm wrestle."

"Oh, dear God," mumbled Will. "I'm a dead man."

Gus smiled kindly and explained that he couldn't possibly take advantage of her like that. He admired her bravery and fidelity to her brother too much to beat her at arm wrestling in front of the entire school.

"Well, if you're scared..." she goaded.

"I'm not scared," Gus countered indignantly.

"You sound scared," said Ella.

"For God's sake, stop!" insisted Will.

But a chant slowly rose from the crowd. "Arm wrestle…arm wrestle…arm wrestle…arm wrestle…" gaining force until the whole alleyway echoed with those words and Gus felt obliged to respect the wishes of his fans.

"Okay!" he announced to a cheer.

A trash can was hastily set up between the little girl and the Swedish mountain. They both rested their elbows on the lid, clasped hands, and when an impartial tenth grader shouted "Go!" Ella slammed the back of Gus's hand into the garbage can lid with an authoritative *doiinnng* that reverberated off the walls of the alley.

The crowd let out an audible, communal gasp. It was over that fast. Gus—and everyone else—stared in stunned amazement. The impossible had occurred. Ella had won.

Rubbing his hurt shoulder, Gus held out his hand and nobly congratulated the victor before turning to Will and saying, "You are lucky to have her as your sister."

"I know," Will responded, striding toward

Gus and boldly taking the bike. "I'll have that now. To the victor go the spoils."

Gus shrugged. "It is only fair. The bike is yours."

But Will didn't want the bike for himself. He rolled it toward Benny and said, "This is for you."

"But I c-c-can't ride," protested Benny.

"Yeah, I'll teach you."

With the eyes of all the gathered students firmly staring at them, Will linked arms with Ella and walked her toward the theater. He leaned into her and whispered, "How the hell did you pull that off?"

Ella smiled, "You know all the goose eggs I've been whipping into omelets, scrambles, and soufflés over the past five days? Well, it's a real workout. And I noticed the other day, I've developed crazy muscles in my right arm. Feel."

Will did. Her arm was like a bulging brick. "Holy crap."

"I know." She giggled. "Lucky he didn't want to arm wrestle leftie. We'd have been in trouble."

Chapter 58

THE THEATER WAS abuzz with people rushing around doing final preparations, including last-minute rehearsals onstage. Ella and Will found Suzanne arranging the painted backdrops.

"Hey, Suzanne," whispered Ella, not wanting to disturb the actors onstage. "Have you met my brother, Will?"

Suzanne looked at him, surprised and impressed at the lack of obvious damage to his face. "Was the fight called off?"

"Ella saved my ass," whispered Will before asking, "Why are the sets all blue? Isn't the musical called *White Christmas*?"

"We said the same thing," replied Suzanne, smiling shyly at Will, who smiled back.

"Sally Kensington made us change them," Ella explained. "Apparently the color blue really makes her eyes pop."

"Oh. Well...they're really good despite being blue," complimented Will, causing Suzanne's cheeks to dial up from a subdued pink to bright red.

"Stop flirting, Will," said Ella, laughing loudly, causing Will's cheeks now to flush red, a thing Ella had never seen before.

"BE QUIEEEEEET!" boomed a voice from the stage. Although they had only been whispering, Sally Kensington marched toward Will, Ella, and Suzanne. In the final days and now hours before curtain time, Sally had become oppressively demanding. "I should have known it would be you, set-painting girl." She poked a finger into Ella's chest.

"Sorry," said Ella, taken aback.

But Sally Kensington was not done. "Your place is in the background. Unheard. *Invisible,* you insignificant, unnecessary, stupid little mouse."

Ella was leaning quite far back, with

Sally's nose inches from her own, when Will stepped in.

"Back off, Kensington," said Will calmly.

Collective chins dropped all around the auditorium. Even Gus Gustavson, who had just entered the theater, felt his mouth fall open. Standing up to Gus showed courage. Standing up to Sally Kensington showed a reckless disregard for one's own personal safety.

"*What* did you say?" Sally whispered, turning her withering gaze onto Will, who swallowed hard but would not be deterred.

Over the past twelve days, Will had been viciously attacked by geese, tracked a partridge through Manhattan, herded cattle, subdued fowl, scraped up and disposed of endless buckets of poop, and had been evicted from his own bedroom. He had been through too much to be intimidated now.

"I said, 'Back off, Kensington.' That's my sister and nobody talks to my sister like that."

Watching Sally Kensington was like watching a volcano as the irrepressible force of gas and hot magma pushed its way up to the top.

You could almost hear the internal rumbling sound.

"Uh, Will," said Ella, pulling at his arm, "I really shouldn't have been so loud during rehearsals..."

"Sally," Will continued, ignoring Ella, "you're a bully. And you have no friends because of it. No real friends anyway because a real friend would have pulled you aside long ago and told you just how insufferable you are."

In the wings, several of the girls Sally considered her closest friends studied their feet and looked up at the ceiling to avoid her gaze.

And now the top flew off the mountain, sending jets of metaphorical hot lava into the air and rolling along the ground where it would incinerate anything in its path.

"GGEEEEEETTTT OOOOOUUUUU-UTTTTTT!!!!!!!!" She screamed at the top of her lungs, the hot air of her breath along with some spittle hitting Will in the face. With the remarkable breath control that comes from years of singing lessons, Sally managed to hold the scream for an impressive thirty seconds of mounting force and volume, her neck veins throbbing and nostrils flaring angrily until...

Have you ever heard the expression "be careful what you wish for"? It means that maybe there are some things that you *think* you really want, but which may be detrimental to you should you actually achieve them. Remember how Sally Kensington was so insistent that the sets be blue so that her eyes would really pop? Well, that's what happened.

Her eyes popped.

At least, it looked like they popped. What in fact happened was that the internal pressure built up by the ferocity and force of her scream caused a blood vessel in each eye to rupture, turning the entirety of the white parts of her eyes a hideous, bright, blotchy red.

"What?!" she questioned those around her watching. "Why are you staring at me like that?!"

A nearby makeup artist handed her a mirror. Sally rarely passed a mirror without taking an admiring look at herself with a satisfied nod of smug approval. But, for the first time in her life, she looked in a mirror and screamed. She looked like a vampire. Like little paintballs of blood had exploded in the whites of her eyes. The effect was quite horrific.

And so—as if frightened by her own reflection—Sally ran. She ran off the stage. Out of the theater. Down the hallway. Through the double doors and disappeared into the street. That was the last anyone saw of Sally Kensington until the new semester began three weeks later and her eyes were finally their usual crystal whiteness again.

Now all eyes landed on Will, who had just caused the lead to abandon the musical. With two hours until curtain time and without Sally Kensington, they were sunk. And yet, rather than blame Will, a cheer rose up from the gathered masses. Even Ms. Conti breathed a sigh of relief as if a heavy weight had been lifted from her shoulders.

Now, however, the musical needed a new lead. And it needed her now. Someone who loved musicals. Someone who had been there for all the rehearsals. Someone who had been watching carefully. Someone who knew every line and every song. Someone who knew every stage direction and movement. Maybe someone who had always been too quiet and shy to stand up for herself but who was now ready to lift her head up high. To shine. To finally be noticed for all the creative brilliance that she possessed.

And, if you just punched the air and shouted, "Hooray for Ella!" you'd be absolutely... wrong.

For starters, Ella had a terrible voice. Truly atrocious. One night, the geese actually *left* the bathroom when she was singing in the shower. And, anyway, Ella was a painter. That's where her creativity lay. Not in singing.

Ella did step forward, though, but only to shout, "Suzanne can do it!" while pushing her timid friend quite literally into the spotlight.

Since the first rehearsals, Ella had noticed Suzanne following Sally's every move, often softly singing along with a gorgeous voice as they painted.

At Ella's urging and with everyone watching in stunned silence, Suzanne opened her mouth and began singing. *"I'm dreaming of a white Christmas…"* The hairs on every arm in the theater stood up on end. And when Gus Gustavson stepped forward to join her, their two voices melted together as deliciously as ice cream and hot caramel.

Chapter 59

WHEN THE CURTAIN rose on that night's performance, there were three remarkable things to note besides Suzanne's awe-inspiring performance. Firstly, in the two hours between the blood vessels in Sally Kensington's eyes exploding and the curtain going up, Ella had turned her attention to the sets and feverishly added to them with a full palette of beautiful colors.

So what the audience saw was not the stripped-down, minimalist, monochromatic blue sets that Sally had insisted on. Rather, they were greeted by bright, joyful, seasonal, multicolored designs full of jolly and whimsical imagery, including drummers, lords, cancan dancers, pipers, and milkmaids.

The second notable event was the arrival in the audience of Henry Sullivan, the man who swore off Christmas five years ago, refusing even to acknowledge its existence, and who studiously avoided all things Christmas-y. And yet here he was at the *Christmas* musical, watching a performance of *White Christmas*. And he was smiling. He was enjoying the performance. And was incredibly proud of all the work done by Ella. Until this very moment, he'd had no idea of the depth of her artistic talents.

But the third thing might have been the most surprising of all. And that was the person sitting next to Henry. It was... Will. Wait. No. That's not surprising at all. Of course Will was sitting on the left of his father. But sitting on the *right* side of Henry, smiling delightfully and showing the charming gap between her front teeth, was Mariana.

Earlier that day, Henry had waited outside of her office, sitting on a damp bench, bundled against the cold and blowing hot air into his hands for warmth. When she finally exited the building he ran up behind her, reaching for her shoulder, when she instinctively spun around, grabbed his outstretched hand, twisted it back on itself, and bent it unnaturally toward his elbow until he was kneeling in a puddle on the pavement, shouting, "Ow ow ow ow ow!" At this point she saw it was Henry, let him up, and apologized.

"It's okay," said Henry, rubbing the blood back into his wrist. "I wasn't sure if you did that because you knew it was me or because you didn't know it was me." He paused and, heartened by a smile that slowly spread across her face, asked, "Could I buy you a coffee?"

They went to a terrible little coffee shop that served weak, burned coffee, where Henry took a deep breath and explained everything. Everything about his wife, her death, his reaction to it, the past five years, his deteriorating relationship with his kids, the dating website, and the mysterious Ms. Truelove who turned their lives upside down by sending, in order, all the gifts from the Christmas carol "The Twelve Days of Christmas," which he found and played for her on his phone, since she was unfamiliar with it. And he did all this without breaking inexplicably into a foreign language or squawking or anything. Needless to say, their coffees were cold by the time he finished. But Mariana's smile was warm.

She told him she certainly understood how they might have thought she was behind everything before reassuring Henry again that she had no idea how to recruit English lords to leap into his garden or where to find can-can dancers. And she loved animals too much to send them to a townhouse in Harlem. Or any other metropolitan center on the eastern seaboard of America.

"It's the school musical this evening," Henry finally said. "Ella painted the sets. So I think I'm going to go. I don't suppose you'd..." He stopped himself. "No, don't worry, it's silly, unless you want, which you wouldn't...I mean, why would you, it'll be...I'm sure you have better, of course you do, doesn't matter, maybe another, because you don't..."

But she placed a hand on his arm, stopping his self-doubting babble to tell him she did and it wasn't silly because she would like to and didn't have anything better and it did matter so why wait for another time?

And that is how Henry ended up in the audience of the school Christmas musical sitting between Will and Mariana.

Chapter 60

NEEDLESS TO SAY, the performance was a huge success. What sort of story would this be if Suzanne froze mutely onstage and then threw up over the front row? Or if everyone found the new backdrops annoyingly distracting and couldn't concentrate on the performances?

Neither of those things happened. In fact, the school newspaper would lead the following issue with a review of the musical, topped by a headline reading in bold capital letters, "SALLY WHO?"

After a number of curtain calls—people lost count—cast and crew shared joyful hugs. Will managed to insert himself in among the celebration and found himself in a congratulatory hug with Suzanne that seemed to mutually linger for longer than a normal embrace. They were just letting go of each other with embarrassed smiles when Gus Gustavson marched up to Ella and, in front of all of the gathered students, instantly turned Ella into something she had never been before: an object of the intense jealousy of almost every girl in the room (and quite a lot of guys).

"Ella, would you like to come over tonight to my family's home for Christmas Eve dinner?"

Everyone knew that Gus lived in a Harlem landmark. It was a vast 1890s match factory that had been abandoned in the 1940s only to sit empty for decades before being completely renovated by Gus's father, a renowned modernist architect.

Ella had seen photos in magazines of the Gustavson home with all of its sleek, minimalist lines, neatly—if not obsessively—clean and uncluttered. Not an unnecessary item in sight. It was quite literally Ella's dream house. Especially in comparison to the current state of her disorderly, cramped, germ-filled house stuffed to the rafters with twenty-three birds, nine cows (including the calf), and fifty total strangers with zero respect for general hygiene or other people's private property.

She looked at Will and Henry, who both indicated their approval. And yet, Ella shook her head, baffling everyone who was watching.

"No. I'd prefer to spend time with my family."

"Maybe another time?" queried Gus magnanimously.

"I'd like that," said Ella, brushing her long hair out of her face and tucking it behind her ear and allowing everyone a clear view of her soft, kind blue eyes.

The Sullivans walked home through the cutting cold of the New York winter evening. Despite the temperature having dropped dramatically, the streets and sidewalks were packed with forgetful people. Some had forgotten to buy their presents until the day before Christmas. Some had forgotten a necessary ingredient for Christmas dinner. And some—maybe, many—had forgotten that they should have told their co-workers and bosses hours ago that it was time to put work behind them in order to spend time with family. The unforgetful people were already at home with family enjoying food, drinks, and gifts, and arguing over what to watch on TV.

Will and Ella walked side by side, nudging each other playfully and giggling at things they mutually found amusing.

Behind them, Henry watched happily. He was happy to be with them. And he was happy because Mariana was walking next to him even though she knew almost every-thing there was to know about him. While he'd been telling her his story earlier that day, he mentally noted at least eleven points where she would have been entirely justified in making an excuse and running away. But here she was. Still with him.

"I've been," she said, "bitten, attacked, charged, stalked, and stomped on by animals. Yet, I still work with them. I don't scare easily."

Henry smiled, "Or...you really just never learn."

Mariana laughed and gave him a playful elbow in the ribs.

After picking up fifteen large pizzas (as there were at home fifty mouths to feed besides their own), the four of them turned the corner onto their street, determined to have a good Christmas Eve no matter what.

They didn't care if the lords were on the roof shooting Henry's first-edition books thrown in the air by the milkmaids. Or if the pipers were roasting meat on a bonfire they'd made in the garden. Or if the drummers had pounded their dining table into splinters. Or if the ladies dancing had brought down the kitchen ceiling with their stomping. Will, Ella, Henry, and Mariana were going to have a good night.

But when they got to their front door, they saw that they should not have been so worried about what destructive acts their guests were engaged in.

Chapter 61

THE HOUSE WAS QUIET.

More than quiet. It was silent.

Not only was there no piping or drumming, there was no squawking, cooing, honking, or mooing. There was no cabaret, polka, or Gilbert and Sullivan light opera to be heard. There were no buckets clanking, feet stomping, teapots pouring, udders emptying, or feathers fluttering. There was no movement at all to be seen through the many broken windows.

Henry twisted his key in the door lock and, with a certain amount of nervous trepidation, gently pushed the door open. The four of them stood at the threshold for a moment, waiting for something or someone to jump out at them. But nothing did.

So they entered the house, listening to the floorboards creak under their footsteps. As they checked the rooms, one by one, they found each one empty of gifts. The destruction they had wrought, however, was certainly still there. The furniture was broken, carpets filthy, drapes torn, walls stained, and bathrooms grimy. The living room, dining room, and kitchen were a junkyard of dirty dishes, glasses, scone plates, portable gas burners, milking stools, smashed eggs, ponchos, and various laundry items still hanging from strings stretched across the rooms. The bricks of butter and vats of milk were still there. And two trays of pastries were still in the oven. As if the cooks had left unexpectedly. In a hurry. Without notice.

"Where did they go?" Mariana whispered.

"I have no idea," whispered Henry, checking the closet for French hens.

"They haven't been gone long," whispered Ella from the living room, where she felt the side of Lord Twitch-Gelding's teapot. "The tea is still warm."

"And ... why are we whispering?" asked Will,

taking the pastries out of the oven, delighted to note that they were baked to perfection at that very moment.

"I don't know," whispered Henry, before clearing his voice and saying loudly, "Anybody here?"

There was not. No people. No birds. No cows.

They went into the garden to check if anyone was still back there. But they discovered that the only gift that still remained was, in fact, the very first gift that had arrived. There, in the dirt, the tree had shattered the pot that once contained it and had taken root in the ground. Despite the cold weather, it had impossibly multiplied in size into a very respectable sapling with limbs covered in rich green leaves and a smattering of white pear blossoms.

"It's beautiful," said Mariana admiringly.

The cold night air, however, drove them all back inside, where, enjoying the solitude and quiet, they ate a little pizza. Mariana pulled a bottle of champagne out of her bag and started to open it, but Henry stopped her, saying that he had decided to lay off booze for a while. Instead, Mariana made hot cocoa for them, which Henry enjoyed more than the finest cognac he'd ever drunk. Maybe because Mariana had made it for him.

Having eaten, Will and Ella were desperate to take advantage of the empty house to wash for the first time in almost a week. Will ran a deep, hot bath and soaked for half an hour while Ella found a pristine, unopened bar of soap in a cupboard and headed for the shower to scrub every bit of dirt and grime off herself.

While the children washed, Henry and Mariana put clean sheets on their beds, which Will and Ella—refreshed, de-stressed, and shiny clean—gleefully dove into. They couldn't remember the last good, comfortable, relaxing, uninterrupted night's sleep they'd had. But they wouldn't think about it for long because they were both enveloped in a heavenly slumber almost before their heads hit the pillows.

On the Day after the
Twelfth Day

Chapter 62

AFTER THIRTEEN GLORIOUS hours of hard-core, dreamy REM sleep, Will and Ella finally peeled themselves off their mattresses. For the first time in twelve days, they had no animal-related chores to rush through or strangers to feed before school, so they luxuriated in every stage between *I-know-I-should-get-up-but-can't* to *I'm-starving-I-wonder-what's-for-breakfast*.

Once up, Ella spent a little time clearing her room of dirty clothes, used towels, and discarded items left by the milkmaids. In his room, Will simply stepped over whatever mess there was on his way into the hallway, where he met Ella exiting her room at the same time.

"Morning." He yawned.

"Morning," concurred Ella. "You think there are any croissants left?"

"I hope so," said Will most sincerely.

But when they went downstairs, they were greeted by a sight more splendid, more delightful, more delicious than mere pastries. For when they descended the stairs, they saw that the entire ground floor of the house was radiant with twinkling, shining, glorious, festive Christmas decorations.

There were ornaments, baubles, boughs of holly, strings of tinsel, bundles of mistletoe, colorful glass balls, and candy canes hanging from everything that offered a place to hang things from.

While Will and Ella had been sleeping, Henry, with Mariana's encouragement and assistance, had brought out multiple dusty, neglected boxes of Christmas ornaments from the very back of a packed closet under the stairs, where they had languished forgotten for five years. Henry and Mariana then spent the next three hours decorating, leaving hardly a surface unadorned. It was as if Henry was trying to make up for the past five years of puritanical restraint by saturating the house with ornamentation now.

While they had been decorating, Mr. Greenblatt, walking his dog, looked in through the front window and saw what they were doing. He went home and brought over a large box of Hanukkah decorations and then rallied the other neighbors to donate whatever they, too, could spare for the cause. The result was a vast cavern of seasonal cheer and lights.

Will and Ella were stunned. In part because they had forgotten it was Christmas Day today. With everything else that had been going on, they had entirely lost track of time.

"It's amazing," sang Ella.

"*You* did this?" asked Will skeptically of his father.

"Me and Mariana," said Henry.

"Yes, but it was his idea," pointed out Mariana. "I just helped."

"Put your coats and boots on," said Henry. "Come see outside."

They followed him out into the garden, where, overnight, a magnificent, thick blanket of snow had fallen, giving the entire outdoor area a magical, fantastic feeling. The weather people's long-promised snow had finally arrived last night while Henry and Mariana were putting strings of lights around trees and bushes and across the garden from fence to fence, causing light to dance and twinkle on pristine whiteness.

"Dad, this is beautiful," whispered Ella.

"I can't take credit for the snow." Henry smiled.

Ella hugged her father and then flopped back onto the ground to make a snow angel. Will paused for a moment and then, abandoning all the detached cool reserve he'd been cultivating for years, gleefully followed suit. The three then embraced until, beckoned by Ella, Mariana joined them in their group hug.

"Wow. Look at that," said Will, pulling away and pointing toward the pear tree. Hanging from one narrow outstretched branch, having seemingly grown from nothing overnight, there was a pear.

One solitary, perfect, juicy pear.

Henry was drawn to it as if by an invisible force. Reaching out, he plucked it from its branch with the gentlest of tugs. He smelled it.

"It's ripe," he said, astonished. And then he took a big bite of it. By the look on his face, it was clear that this was the sweetest, most succulent pear he had ever tasted. That is, until he nearly cracked a tooth on something hard inside of it. Holding his hand up to his mouth, he let something drop into his palm.

"Ew, Dad," said Ella, unaware of what he was doing.

But Henry said nothing and simply held up what he'd bitten from the *inside* of the pear.

It was a key.

"A key?" puzzled Will.

Glistening with spit and fruit juices was a small, simple key that had somehow grown *inside* of the pear.

Over the previous twelve days, the Sullivans had become habituated—blasé even—about the extraordinary, the inexplicable, and the magical. But this was the strangest thing of all. A key inside of a pear on a pear tree, which, against all the laws of horticulture, had grown to fruit-bearing maturity overnight in the dead of winter.

"It's the key to what?" asked Mariana.

"I have no idea," replied Henry.

Over the following half hour, they tried the key in every lock in the house. Drawers, windows, padlocks, boxes, clocks. But the little key didn't fit anywhere. When all possibilities were exhausted, Ella sat up brightly.

"I think I know," she said and disappeared upstairs.

A moment later she returned clutching a dusty blanket, which she carefully unfolded to reveal the ballerina music box they had discovered in the attic. Turning it over to reveal the slot, Henry introduced the key, which slid in perfectly. He then took a breath and slowly twisted the key three or four times before letting go and setting the box on the table.

The music began to play and the ballerina gracefully began to turn. Finally, they could breathe a sigh of relief, each remembering the tune again and, with it, a personalized memory of Katie Sullivan, their mother and wife.

Ella remembered a time before her cleanliness obsession when she and her mother painted messily in her room, smudging colors freely over paper and themselves while the ballerina spun and played softly in the background. Will remembered the tune playing while his mom gently rubbed his back as he drifted off to sleep. And Henry remembered the adoring look on his wife's face when she accidentally knocked it off the table and Henry caught it before it smashed on the floor.

In that moment one thing became clear to all three Sullivans: that Will and Ella's mother was the only person who could have subjected them to everything they'd been through in the past twelve days. She was the only person who could have known that this is what it would take to shake the family out of its downward spiral of apathy and detachment.

It was impossible, of course, but everything about the past twelve days had been impossible. Why not the person behind it, too? Who else cared enough about them to put them through the trials and tribulations of the past twelve days? Who else knew that they needed something extreme to get them off of their errant, divergent paths and bring them back together as a unified family? Who else knew that, deep down, they would be able to survive anything thrown at them?

Watching their dreamy expressions of contentment, Mariana guessed correctly that the music box must have belonged to . . . me, Katie Sullivan . . . Will and Ella's mom . . . Henry's wife . . . or, as they've been calling me throughout this story, Ms. Truelove.

Epilogue

HENRY SAT AT his computer. Ms. Truelove's profile page from Splice.com was on the screen. He had been staring at the enigmatic, silhouetted profile photo. Only now did he recognize the distinctive curve of her cheek created by a whimsical smile he remembered so well. Only now did he see the soft swoop of her neck into the sculptural shoulder he had kissed a million times. The clues had been there all along if he'd only been clear-headed enough to take the time to open his mind and look.

The cursor blinked impatiently in the message box. He wanted to write something. He'd had no trouble writing before. But, without the fuels of anger and sarcasm, the words

seemed unable to form. His fingers seemed
unable to move. He tried to organize his
hoard of thoughts and emotions. Eventually
he distilled them into two words. Once those
two words were out, the rest of his sentiments
were set free.

Don't go.

Wherever you are, however you've been
here, don't leave.

I know the twelve days of Christmas
are over. I know the gifts from the carol
have been given. I know that Will, Ella,
and I are a family once again.

But that doesn't mean you can go.
That doesn't mean that we don't need
you anymore. We do. I do. You saw
how useless I was without you. I
mean...you had to come back from
the dead to help me. That's how bad
I was!

Henry paused and looked around the room.

Are you still here?...Can you see
us?...Can you hear us?

Henry paused again. For a sign. A message.
A something. Maybe a knocking sound or for
the lights to flicker. But there was no sign. So
he began typing again.

Katie...I'm sorry I let you down. I let
your death suck the life out of me. But,
my dear true love, I promise you I won't
let it happen again. You live on in Will
and Ella. You live on in my heart, my
soul, and in every breath I take.

Thank you for loving me. Thank you
for teaching me the meaning of true
love. The few precious years we had
together were filled with more joy and
laughter than most get in a lifetime.
For that, I consider myself a very lucky
man, even if you were taken away from

me at the beginning of what surely was meant to be a long and magnificent life together.

Our story was cut short and will remain unfinished forever. But even in its incomplete state, it is…exquisite and perfect. And that, too, is how it will remain forever.

Henry wiped a drop of moisture from his eye and then let out a little laugh.

Y' know, my true love, the past twelve days have been so utterly bizarre, I might be inclined to think that they'd been nothing more than an outlandish, preposterous fever dream…if it weren't, of course, for the complete destruction of the house. Seriously. You couldn't have shaken me out of my funk without turning the house into a cross between Noah's ark and Grand Central Station?

Katie...be free. Enjoy whatever comes
next after this life. We'll be fine even if
we miss you every millisecond of every
moment of every hour of every day.

You will always be in our hearts,

Henry

He pressed SEND.

Sitting back in his chair, he rubbed his eyes, ran his fingers through his hair, and stretched. Leaning forward again to close the window on his screen, he paused for a moment in the hope that the little envelope symbol on the Splice website might light up, indicating that Ms. Truelove...Katie...had responded. But it remained unilluminated. Of course. Because everything about the past twelve days had been to prove to Henry that he and Will and Ella could pull together and be a happy family without her. That it was okay to move on.

Taking another deep breath, he decided to scroll to the bottom of the page, and, with resignation, he hovered the cursor over the Delete Account button. He thought for a moment and then clicked gently on it. And turned off the computer altogether.

Henry was ready for bed. He would not get up again until every atom in his body was recharged and ready to begin the next chapter of his life. He didn't know what that chapter would look like. He didn't know where that chapter would be set. He didn't know who—besides Will and Ella—would be in that chapter with him. But as he considered his future and wondered if he'd done the right thing in deleting the account, he noticed something on a shelf behind the desk. It was the long, narrow velvet box from *Groot Liefde & Co.* the jewelers. Henry had assumed the gold rings had disappeared at the same time as all the other gifts. But there the box was, still in the house. He reached out and held it for a moment before flipping the lid open to see that three of the rings had indeed disappeared. But two remained. One large men's-size gold band. And one slightly thinner, more delicate women's gold band.

He jumped when there was a knock on the door and Mariana's head popped in. "Everything okay?" she inquired brightly.

Henry snapped the box shut and smiled. He knew it would be. And, as with everything else good in his life, he knew he owed it to Ms. Truelove.

About the Authors

James Patterson is the world's bestselling author. His enduring fictional characters and series include Alex Cross, the Women's Murder Club, Michael Bennett, Maximum Ride, Middle School, and Ali Cross, along with such acclaimed works of narrative nonfiction as *Walk in My Combat Boots, E.R. Nurses,* and his autobiography, *James Patterson by James Patterson.* Bill Clinton *(The President Is Missing)* and Dolly Parton *(Run, Rose, Run)* are among his notable literary collaborators. For his prodigious imagination and championship of literacy in America, Patterson was awarded the 2019 National Humanities Medal. The National Book Foundation presented him with the Literarian Award for Outstanding Service to the American Literary Community, and he is also the recipient of an Edgar Award and nine Emmy Awards. He lives in Florida with his family.

Tad Safran is a storyteller who has written for some of the biggest companies in TV, film, podcasts, newspapers, and books, always with the same goal: to entertain, intrigue, and amuse. He lives at the top of a hill with his wife and twin sons who make every day feel like Christmas, i.e. loud, messy, hectic, exhausting and quite wonderful.

For a complete list of books by

JAMES PATTERSON

VISIT
JamesPatterson.com